American Stories

Prose Series 28

Pierre-Yves Pépin

American Stories

Guernica

Toronto / New York

1996

Antonio D'Alfonso, editor
Guernica Editions Inc.
P.O. Box 117, Station P, Toronto (Ontario), Canada M5S 2S6
340 Nagel Drive, Cheektowaga, N.Y., 14225-4741 USA

Legal Deposit — Third Quarter
National Library of Canada

Library of Congress Catalog Card Number: 94-77151

Canadian Cataloguing in Publication Data
Pépin, Pierre-Yves, 1930-
American stories
(Prose Series; 28)
ISBN 0-920717-96-9
I. Title. II. Series.
PS8581.E618Z53 1994   C813'.54   C93-090050-2
PQ3919.2.P46Z465 1994

Table of Contents

At different periods of time during the writing and rewriting of my stories, many people have been helpful with their criticisms and suggestions to improve the manuscript. Special thanks to Sharleen Rains, John Mahoney and Roberto Ozores. The three of them, all born in the United States, now live and are professionally active in Montreal or thereabouts.

A Vietnam Vet on the Road

I pass by baldy and smoggy El Paso at four o'clock in the afternoon. Two hours later, I reach the beautiful waters of Amistad Reservoir. Wide Pecos River depressed between whitish flat walls of a deep gorge. Strong landscape. Dusk. Flanked by bags, suitcases and cardboard boxes, a guy is standing near a bridge. What is he doing there? I cross the bridge. After landing on the other side of Pecos River, I decide to cross the bridge again. Half turn. I do it. It is almost dark now. The guy, slim and in his thirties, is still there. I realize only now that he is hitchhiking. Take him with me. We drive to Sanderson. Both hungry. We dine on my wallet. Piles of hamburgers. Cold foaming beer. Full moon shining on bizarre rocks wind-pierced and pitted. Deep innocent sleep.

The good sun wakes me up. My road companion has slept nearby, in an abandoned shack. We run, and run, and run. Desert feelings, Mexican feelings. Sparse bushy vegetation. A lot of tumbleweed moving on sand, plus dry rivers and creeks. Like mysterious Japanese black ink drawings, a ranch portal with nothing beside, with absolutely nothing

7

around. Here and there, trains dotting the plains. All merchandise convoys. Four engines pulling each of them — when they move! Many just doze for hours. Under a boiling mid-day sun. An incredible number of coyotes, rabbits, skunks and other non-identified small and medium-sized wild animals, flattened on the road. Tireless vultures patrolling the skies.

Garry tells me he was a helicopter's rear gunner in the Vietnam War — the average life-time of a rear gunner in combat was less than a minute. Most of the suffering of that silly and devilish period still seems to inhabit Garry. What can I say? After twenty-four hours to-gether in the van, the vet jumps off at a crossroads. Las Cruces. Road Number 25 North. I am heading for Sante Fe, New Mexico. Road Number 10 West for him, California next. Garry has done some work as a marine engine mechanic, in Florida, and is going back home. Regardless of the place, of the geographic loca-tion, home strongly means Tammy, his wife. She is expecting a baby.

I stop the motor of the van. A lot of words pop out in a quick flow. Both sides. The air is light. Why split here?

'You are a real pioneer, you are full of flesh, you are a very distinguished per-son . . . ,' and so forth. 'I think that I will name my son Pedro.'

I race the engine. The reverberation of the sun on the sand, on the road, on the mobile homes turning their back on the Pacific Coast, and on everything ready to shine, is burning my eyes. Where are you now, Garry . . . brother.

Pow! Pow!

Splendid, magnificent, the imposing mountains, fourth dimension brought by the moving shadows related to a sun running swiftly towards the bottom of a dry slope, the Apache country is all around. Road 70 crossing southwest Arizona, Bylas, Geronimo, and so on. Pickups shining with bright colors are rolling at moderate speeds. They are packed with Indians seated, backs straight, on the floor of the rear boxes.

Men's hats half-dropped over the eyes; dressed in dark clothes, their faces are like copperplate engravings. Colorful kerchiefs knotted over women's dark gray hair. Like flags and flames. These kerchiefs weave in the early evening breeze. The people seated on the floor of the rear boxes are looking towards a remote point which seems close to the infinite.

Eden. Very small place. I halt in front of a lonely country store, one of many dotting the road. The purpose of the halt is to buy some food. Half dead from drinking alcohol, two Indians are rolling in the dust. Their endless legs are covered by torn and stained jeans. I just can't stand to see them kicking desperately towards the sky. The front door of the country store is quickly opened by a nervous hand and . . . slam! It's cool inside. Feet covered with cowboy boots down at the heels, the guys are still kicking in the open air, outside.

The Alligator Farm
and the Ostrich Prey

Saint Augustine in October. The day following a very heavy night storm. A so-called Alligator Farm stands beside the town. One of the daily shows is now taking place. I cross the ticket counter turnstile just in time. A guy dressed in a spick-and-span khaki suit is busy in the middle of a rustic amphitheatre. The swash-buckler is opening a 'gator's mouth with strong arms. It's all blades and swords inside. A slow-motion 'fight' starts between Man and Beast. The performing artist works hard. *Clic-clic* . . . *Clic-clic.* The photographers are firing all around. The snapshots will illustrate for post-erity each and every one of the absurd molest-ing tricks. The 'curtain' drops right after the victory of Man. But I am not through with the shows.

The bell rings again. Act Two. Snake circus now. Searching fun at any cost, the visitors gather again. Cottonmouth snakes, rattle-snakes, coral snakes twist in front of the audience: no problem, there is a glass plate between them and us. The new artist-performer, a sturdy man, is lecturing just like a scholar in a school class. At one point in the interminable bla-bla-bla, he forces some rattle-snakes to ejaculate their venom into small bottles. Final hint, he drives all the rattlers crazy. Shaking their tails angrily, the frenzied reptiles emit a frightening strident noise. More. The *agent provocateur* acts in such a way that — one by one — those deadly musicians bite his heavy leather boots. I feel tense, I have enough, the show is over. Satisfied and smiling spectators quickly disperse. Some, still strolling around; others, leaving right away. I stay.

While drifting here and there in an almost deserted area of the Alligator Farm, I notice something big and heavy suddenly move fast, close to my back. I freeze. A fabulous chicken six feet high, beak open, approaches on loose gravel. Small head perched on long neck, vicious evil-minded eyes. Its bald ass, as indecent as a caged monkey's ass, is flanked with pink-colored thighs; it is an ostrich. An ostrich who seems fully determined to revenge right on the spot all the barbecued and stewed gallinaceus of the whole world. Destiny had happened to choose a poor roadrunner as the propitiatory victim. I pinch my arm vigorously to make sure that I am not living a nightmare. My arm hurts and the ostrich keeps on moving. The jogging style of the charger is something frightening. Ah! The gait, the dreadful gait of a blind mechanic, of an automat. Razor-blade-like spurs implant in the big mud pies of the pawns. The eyes! Their flaming beacons aimed at my flickering ones as if the stern bill will pluck them in a jiffy.

Shaky. Try to back up. One foot, two feet, a wire fence scratches my shoulders painfully. Half-crazy, half-paralyzed. Close to panic. Desperate feeling of being trapped. But the zoo parade is not over. Two close relatives of the former aggressor — an emu and a casoar — are dryly pacing to and fro nearby. Prickling up and down my spine. Cold sweat running all over my body. I turn my head around. Still nobody. Tourists all gone. Not even an attendant loafing. Anyway, the translation-transmission in plain words of what I am now experiencing with these devilish beasts would surely be a tricky business! From one side, I know precisely where I am. From the other side, I feel totally lost. Flashing blackout. Primal scream and zoom all over.

On the revulsed retina of a well-fed dog moving lazily along the alley, there remained that day the image of a foolish man who yelled and gesticulated as if he had a ball of fire in the seat of his pants. Balancing himself on the top of a garbage bin, a black bird took the relay and watched the remainder of the one-man-show safari. Spasmodically patting on his way out of the dark and stone-like carapace of a Galapagos turtle shining under a plain Florida sun, the bearded running-jumping biped crossed a gangway stretched over an artificial marsh. But as the marsh was entertaining a full crowd of respectful senior citizen alligators, the hosts, excited by the yelling, opened and closed their big mouths at the speed of a machine-gun shooting. *Snap! Snap! Snap!*

The last visitor for that beautiful day in October in Saint Augustine, disappeared at the speed of a comet. Out of the gate now. Running to find his Dodge van. One, two, one, two, the lonely *clap clap* of the leather sandals could be heard on the civilized, asphalted parking lot. Noise of a car engine diminishing quickly. Peace back again to the 'gator farm. Everybody inside is now free to go back to their personal business and routine.

Monsieur Hulot, California Style

Calistoga. Municipal tennis courts on a winter Saturday morning. Very middle-class. Arms and legs of most weekenders are brawny and vigorous. But bodies, shaped by milk-and-meat diet, chubby. I look around. Only 'registered' couples all over the place! The hard-surfaced balls slam and rebound on the cracked greenish asphalt. Me, what am I doing there, alone? A twisted racket in my right hand, I scratch the back of my head with the left. No partner. The manager-lady of the Chicanos cabins where I live, my supposed-to-be partner, has changed her mind at the very last minute.

Growing, growing irritation. Why do I stay? I start to shoot over a deserted net and walk towards the other side. Two shots again. The first one is an ace. The second ball is weak but good. I cross the court another time. And again, and again . . . A full hour like that. Boiling, boiling inside. I finally leave the court the way I came. Very serious, not a penny of good humor in my pocket, and still alone.

It is only on Sunday that I start to laugh. Even today, it is not over. Just imagine that! Just look at the guy! A white cotton hat shaped like a piss-pot encircled by a narrow rim topping a genuine hairy hobbit head. Khaki shorts, very old style. Long legs whose feet are shod with a pair of antediluvian Adidas yawning at the front, yawning at the back, not to mention the dampness victim, I mean the twisted racket and the whimsical sinusoidal curves transmitted to each and every tennis ball shot by a boiling frustrated *hurluberlu*. I recognize in that robot-picture Monsieur Hulot, the movie hero created by French moviemaker Jacques Tati. Yes, the European comic suddenly appeared on my mental screen. It was him, no doubt. But Californian in style, of course.

New Year's Eve, 1980, According to *The San Francisco Chronicle*

On the second day of January 1980, the sun was not shining at all over Frisco and the rain was not far from pouring all over the place. Got up happy that day. Yeah, got up happy but did a very unwise thing. Bought the last edition of a newspaper and started to swallow the pieces right away:

> Thousands of New Year's Eve revellers were involved in the worst rioting in the history of Reno. — The barges, one carrying a cargo of odd deadly liquefied gas, remained beached on the Marine Coast. — Afghans mobbed the Soviet Embassy in Teheran to protest the Kremlin's intervention in Afghanistan. — A fire during a New Year's party in a rural Quebec town killed at least 42 persons and injured 50. — A chemical in the sweat of men is apparently attractive to women and may be used in an aftershave lotion. — A strong quake struck the Azores

in the mid-Atlantic, crumbling buildings and killing at least 52 persons.

That was the front page. Funny sparkles swung in my head and my knees began to shake like an accordion played by a drunken Russian sailor. So I stooped, buttocks resting on heels, and dug inside the thrilling masterpiece of the horror picture show. Fully terrorized and hypnotized, wanting to know more.

Monoxide fumes kill four in Texas (San Antonio). — Violent New Year in San Francisco. — A couple's precarious ordeal (Car accident in Philadelphia). — Push to reopen marine's glacier tomb to hikers (Mount Rainier Park). — Dense fog, drizzle in the Bay Area. — Huge crowd-slaying arrests at the Rose Bowl Parade (Pasadena). — One person was slain and nearly 100 were arrested along the route of the 91st. — Quake gambler loses his bet (Las Vegas: taken 70/1. He forecast an earthquake in 'Frisco between midnight and 8 am. on January 1st). — Kansas City getting back its firemen. — Ugly man tells of plan for murder (A Chicago guy; to be carried out in Los Angeles during the holiday period. Because he is *ugly* and nobody loves him). — BART arson probe: teenager held (Tried to set fire to a car. In San Francisco. Seventeen years old). — On the beach (Two pictures covering two-fifths of the page about the chlorine

barge. There were already two or three pictures of the very same barge on the front
page). — Sweet and sour notes at Quentin.
— Muggers stab and strip archbishop
(Porto Allegre, Brasil). — Judge reviewing
terrorists' case (Chicago).

Except for the ads, there was nothing else
on pages two to five of the *San Francisco
Chronicle*. I rubbed my eyes then began to feel
so much anger that I tore my newspaper apart
with both hands and my remaining teeth.
Several people quickly gathered around. There
were two winos, a female cop, a jogger and a
nun. The wind from the Pacific Ocean had
blown away most of the pages but there were
still a few left, dispersed and dancing erratically
between the cars, the bikes and the baby carriages. I was still chewing the front page when
the astonished passers-by encircled me. The
faces of these people expressed a genuine feeling of compassion. After a short lapse of time,
in a single voice, just like a chorus, they all
said, 'Here is a perfect case of overdose.'

What with one thing and another, lunchtime had come. They all left the scene but the
nun. The female cop distributed free-of-charge
tickets to passers-by and tried hard at the same
time to fix a date with someone — male or
female — for the night; the jogger shadow-
boxed while expelling a kind of tantric *OM*; the
two winos begging for a shave, a hot dog and

20

a pint. When the last member of the too-short-lived chorus was seen disappearing into a streetcar full of stupid tourists sucked from all the boring suburbs of the world, the nun took the lead in the situation. Lasciviously sliding both arms under my armpits, then taking a firm painful grip, she helped me back on my feet with a small but warm kiss on my sweating neck.

And there we went. Down the hill. To the old and venerable convent. For a bowl of first-class mushroom soup. A pink and black novice was reading aloud with a lot of tremolos, glissandos and a few gurgling staccatos, in the stinky refectory dominated by an old prima donna famous in the soap operas of her time. The pink and black novice was reading *The Apocalypse According to Saint John the Beloved*, for the benefit of the whole pious company sneering around the table. Then I had a fit. Totally against my will, I broke the soup bowl with my teeth. The novice kept on reading with her sweet, mild voice. I stole a not-too-fresh custard pie, picked a pocket-sized Bible on the way out, and found myself shivering in the cold winter rain.

All wet from top to bottom in a few seconds. I was downtown again. A veteran wino clothed in rags, a war medal ribbon pinned on a dirty overcoat, stinking like hell but smiling like an angel, piggy red eyes and bulbous red nose flashing, passed by and gave me his paper hat constructed from numerous sheets of a newspaper. I checked the name just before covering my big head. It was a wet and fresh copy of the *San Francisco Chronicle* for the second day of January, 1980.

The Bloodsuckers
and the Apple Offering

The big eight-cylinder is steaming. Tucson. Parking alongside a city public park done in style. Lunch hour. I open the side door of the van to cook something, but I hesitate. I am not hungry at all for the moment. Too much driving in the morning. Close the doors and decide to walk on the green and get some exercise to ease stomach and belly muscles. Tough sun. Even in the middle of November. Take a walk in a zig-zag pattern to stay in the shadow of the trees. A whole bunch of people, all kinds and sizes, are waiting in a line for something to eat. What about food stamps? Go closer.

Two guys, two yellow monks Far East style, are serving curry rice garnished with greenish bits of cabbage. Walk around the spot two or three times, then find myself in line just like everyone else. Like everyone else but a bit ashamed of it, at first. A tall man in front of me. My nose doesn't go over his shoulders. Dressed in straight jeans and wool shirt, slim, eyes filled with disillusion. Speaks briefly with his lady companion. She is dressed about the same way as the man. Both are in their late fifties. I kill time resting on one leg, then the other. Someone, unseen, is talking to me from behind. I half turn my head. A thin, medium-sized man is just behind, looking at me through small round glasses.

He is poorly dressed and wears light boots. Pathetic black boots, very old fashion. Narrow and laced high on the ankles, they are just like the ones one sees on those brownish daguerre-otypes of the late nineteenth century. Yes, the boots are real antiques, but the man, John, not much older than thirty. The waiting line has shortened. Hungry now. Our turn finally comes and we get steamy carton plates full of the above-mentioned delicacies. We do not eat in a hurry, even though John has an appoint-ment. Tucson Plasma Donor Station located at 300 Congress; corner of Fifth Avenue is the target. Yes, he sells blood sometimes. His own, of course.

In Los Angeles and El Paso, recently. The last place — a borderline area — was crowded with poor Chicanos. The blood donor station is a popular spot down there. And as in other towns, this station probably attracts winos. Roomy place. Fifty chairs to keep people com-fortable while a pipeline needle is firmly pinched in one arm. A business: one trades about four hours of attendance for ten bucks. And the very same volume of blood is resold for one hundred. Last Friday, on November

9th, 1979, while John was donating, three seated people fainted.

We are still hungry. I don't believe that free rice splashed on carton plates is very nourishing, even garnished with greenish cabbage chips. We go back in line for a second serving. It is swallowed quickly, while we are seated among other clients, chatting and relaxing. Harassed by hundreds of pigeons — Oh God! I hate those dirty fat birds full of deadly germs — we leave the park quickly after a few minutes. Sun still tough, one o'clock in the afternoon. On our way out of the park, I have no difficulty convincing John to forget about the local blood donor station. At least for a few days . . . Instead of the cancelled appointment, we plan a city tour. Brain loaded with the story of the El Paso blood donor's case, and with others of the same desperate kind, my degree of happiness is quite low. Anyway, we go here and there in Tucson. Visiting an old Spanish church, browsing through a second-hand bookstore, sightseeing the nice female clerks on a plaza at coffee break, and so on.

While loafing on the hot sidewalk, we see a divine young lady pop out of the laundromat, baby secure in her arms. Very tall, smiling, here comes Barbara. I do not know what she has on her mind this day. I do not know if we look like sinners whose souls are filled with hundreds of crimes, but what I do know is that she sparks onto a first-class preaching master-piece as soon as the civilities are over. Sin, hell, heaven, the Coming of Jesus, she throws the whole gamut over our head and shoulders. John keeps still; not me! One hundred per cent cynical about this Tibetan prayer-drummer-like circus. I am ready to react bluntly.

I will not! Her fresh innocence and defenceless opening cool down my red hot ver-bal weapons. Those weapons evaporate in a jiffy. Then, surprising myself, I suddenly jump in the van parked nearby, and rummage swiftly in the food box. Come back to John, to the baby, and to Barbara. No words. My face flushed. I offer a big red apple to the lady . . . This irrational move, according to my well-tested rigid behavior standards, will change the mood of two guys for the whole day. For the better.

A First-Class Racer
and the Barracuda

Four, five feet of water. A comfortably sized, half-round crab is shaking, digging and threatening the seabed's plant carpet. Lots of small fish surrounding the big guy. What the hell are they fooling around for? From place to place, a yellow spot of sand reflects the aqua sun. I paddle a little farther, moving lazily. Knife-shaped, a fish created by God to cut his likenesses in pieces passes by. Six feet of water. I recognize a few tropical fish with their globular eyes, the kind sold in pet shops at home and put in aquariums the size and shape of a pumpkin. But the well-known miniatures are one foot long here!

The underwater morning parade keeps on moving. Silver fish singularize themselves with a mackerel tail. Other ones, leaf-shaped, reflect all the delicate shades of a beautiful month of September. Jewfish imprisoned in a scaled corset, small translucent squid and so on, the show is first class. Wow! A pouch-like swimmer, vertically striped with a wide orange stroke of brush, flashes by just under my nose.

My random movements take me near the shadow of something huge. I see the wrecked pier lying at the end of White Street in Key West. Follow the submerged structure with care, lengthwise. A school of opalescent fish moves swiftly between rusted beams coated with spongy green stuff.

Pop my head out of the water. Clean the diver's mask with saliva. Three sea birds are perched on an armed cement slab showing all its twisted and rusted rods. They stare at me with cold glances. The hell with those son-of-a-bitches! I dive briskly, my frog-like paddles waving and splashing water all around. Eight feet of water and the far end of the pier. The open sea is just there. I don't have to go far to understand what it might really mean. A bulky barracuda moves slowly under me. The worst thing is that he acts as if he does not see me at all. Yet I know well that this hypocrite has spotted me perfectly.

I visualize myself as a tantalizing pink sea worm, wriggling for the benefit of a huge specimen of the local marine fauna. Dinnertime for the terrific sea tiger? Will it be drama or vaudeville? The barracuda keeps pace and direction towards deep sea. So long, monster. No drama, no vaudeville, no butcher's business, but — as a rain check — a plain sporting event takes place right on the spot. Usually belittle myself as a swimmer. Just became a first-class racer that day. Shore side.

The Marine's Cemetery
on Point Loma

When I was living near San Diego, I used to go to Point Loma quite often. From there you can see North Island Naval Air Force Station on Coronado Peninsula; a Naval Supply Center on Point Loma itself; a large area of San Diego; and, of course, the Pacific Ocean. A beautiful area. The sun has to be seen when it sets.

Last time I was there, the 'All Aboard for the Orient Cosmic Solar Express' sung by a flock of white and black sea birds, pierced the fresh air at exactly five-thirty post meridiem. Close to the horizon line — a line heavily shaded by numerous clouds — the sun quickly lost its circular shape. First, it was redesigned like a vase or an Indian turban. Second, it deformed like a balloon being punctured. The phenomenon was astonishingly realistic. Anyone loafing around could most probably hear the *hiss*.

For the visitor using Scenic Drive 209 connecting Freeway Number 5 from San Diego, there is no problem at all finding Point Loma. Through Fort Rosecrans Military Reserve and the cemetery, it takes you directly to the historical lighthouse.

On a beautiful Sunday, winter 1980, I really looked at the cemetery for the first time. Forty thousand military people resting in peace for eternity. Most of them very young when they died. Resting in peace . . . for eternity. All alike. Forty thousand little white cairns settled in a geometric pattern of rows. All in ranks. All of them ready for the parade of the Last Judgement. Nothing to do. Just waiting.

My heart suddenly starts to beat loudly. No, I do not agree! They are not dead. They are just quiet kids gone for a long night of sleep . . . no noise. The passing cars are far away. Just a soft sea breeze. Strange feeling invading me. The earth is pulsing at Point Loma! The rocky and rugged peninsula has become a wide chest expressing the love needs of the sleeping kids. Compassion overwhelms me like a summer moon tide. Sun shines with a cruel brilliance over the little white cairns dotting the clean-cut green grass.

But the emotion soon transforms itself. An uncomfortable feeling is now coming from all around. The situation is difficult to bear. It is as if the kids would be unhappy with me. Me doing nothing for them. Me ready to leave them. Chilled. Pretty sure that I have disappointed them in some way. Time to depart. Follow Scenic Drive 209 connecting with Freeway Number 5, and so on. Even today, I am not at all sure if it would be possible to go back around Fort Rosecrans National Cemetery and keep cold blood.

Picked Up Three Indians in a Row

From Cameron, Arizona, the best road is 89 North. The whole area is a compound of dry and rocky desert. Belongs to the Navahos. So, it does not surprise me that the young Indian I have picked up on my way is a member of the famous tribe. He is an electrician employed in Tuba City. Going there now for his usual day of work. Very short drive. Leave him at a crossroad. There is another Navaho, an elderly person, standing in the very same place. Plumpish, black hat low on his forehead, he is waiting for a vehicle to take him along. Just back from the dentist's chair in Tuba.

A Pepsi can in one hand, he does not speak much. To tell the truth, he does not speak at all. But after about half an hour, he starts to mumble from time to time, while we are rolling along at moderate speed. I understand absolutely nothing of his small talk. Anyway, busy with my driving, I do not care too much. Eventually look at him when he starts to gesticulate soberly. We are approaching Page now. The Indian points to the side door with one hand.

Stop the van. Turn the ignition off. The old man walks out. The soft drink can is full of blood. His mouth too. Cleans both. On the road again.

Near the beginning, or the end if you prefer, of Lake Powell. Noon. Sandwiches and raw food swallowed in the parking lot of the dam's reservoir. The sun is nothing but a ball of fire. Let's move out of here and quick! Heat haze on the road. Maybe the haze is a mirage in my mind, but one thing is sure, the road is damned hot. Not a car in sight. I drive fast. That is not wise for the mechanic of the vehicle. The hard blue of the water of the reservoir is shining like an acrylic painting. No boat on the lake, but a lonely guy walking in the same direction as I roll.

Slow down the van. Middle-aged and bulky, bare head, he continues walking straight ahead. Stare at him. Gosh, another Indian! He asks for nothing though. It does not matter. I can't stand leaving him in such a furnace. Tell the poker-faced guy to come in the van. No words. He jumps briskly and there we go. A Sioux from North Dakota. Had worked as a farmhand, down south. Going back home now. Not too much information gathered beyond that. Cruising speed 55 m.p.h. The heat decreases. We are travelling in a less deserted area now. The road also becomes a little more busy. State line. Leaving Arizona and entering Utah, just before Kanab. Road 89 winds through a narrow valley flanked with trees. Archaic houses just like in the old times.

My passenger is still with me. Had begun to hear voices! At first I do not care at all. This country is a free country, isn't it? So . . . But soon after we pass Kanab, the mood change in the van. Staring at the outside mirror, passenger's side, the Sioux starts to mumble. Even asks me to stop. Still in a fair humor I do so. He steps down and checks carefully around the vehicle so as to be sure that his friends are not playing nearby to fool him. Returns to his seat. We roll again.

Heavy atmosphere building up now. Paranoia acute. Crude aggression shown in the passenger's seat. Worries invade driver's seat. The Sioux mumbles some more. Becomes febrile and sweats heavily. Too many magic mushrooms, I realize quite late. Thick air. I am sweating now too. Panguitch. Nice town of Panguitch in sight. Rough stop right in the middle of business area. Tell the goddam guy to get out. He slams the door and right away looks for a place to hide. The Devil eat him! Throw away with rage my symbolic Good Samaritan hat. Take a deep breath and turn the ignition key. I figure I'll drive alone for the remaining portion of the journey. Up to Salt Lake City. Hope you don't mind.

Young Couple
Abandoned
in Grand Canyon

The Grand Canyon, in the geographical my-
thology of any genuine American, is considered
one of the greatest marvels of the world. You
have the very same dreams about going there
during your terrestrial life, as a Muslim does
about visiting Mecca. Sixth day of November,
1979. Nourished by that moving feeling, I am
driving westbound on Freeway 40. My day ride
begins in Santa Fe, early morning. Discreet
humming of wind on van's sides. Driving
steady at 55 m.p.h. I am inhabited by the firm
idea of accomplishing a sacred pilgrimage to
the Grand Canyon. The energizing feeling
stemming from it remains strong up to Gallup.
Right after, the combined depressive action of
rain mixed with ice, and of the panoramic sight
of snow dusted over the nearby mountain
ridges, changes my mood. The Grand Canyon
idea transforms itself into a solid burden at
Flagstaff.

So — no shame, no surprise — after a
warm and filling dinner at a nearby truck stop,

I go straight to Phoenix. That goes for my attempt during the fall. Springtime 1980. Early April. Very same Freeway 40. Driving eastbound from Utah. In good spirits, the desire to pay a visit to the Grand Canyon is high again. But bad weather is building up. Again . . . Cold, strong winds. The mobile homes on the road are swaying as much as the gondolas at Disneyland. An old lady drives one of these monsters. Her head crowned with shaking hair curlers, she is glued to the steering wheel. When I speed up and pass, she glances down at me through her thick glass. Insulted, angry, stupid, terrified. The hell with her!

One hundred and eighty miles before arriving in Flagstaff, Kingsman. Sightseeing drive, loop drive in Hualapai Indian territory. No vehicles on the narrow road but my Dodge van. Barren landscape, desolate landscape. Rusty fallen signs from the forties and fifties. Insolent scarecrow along the road? No, just old gas pump out of use and maybe never used. Peach Springs, Seligman. The weather has changed her grade from fresh to cold. Throw my exotic leather sandals in the back of the van. Wool socks and boots. Warmest sweater drawn out of the clothes trunk. Then a winter cap. Conifers. Snow spots under tree cover. Stunt, dry and gray winter affects the vegetation. I glance at the mountains . . . I think they are topped with 'local' rain storms. Oh yeah! That is real snow.

Back on Freeway 40. Williams. Buy and re-place front shock absorbers at a Chevron serv-ice station. Sun goes down. Beautiful colors on everyting. Those colors are crude. Just like in the Arctic. From Williams, a road goes straight down to Grand Canyon, south rim side. This time I go. It will be sixty miles in one shot. The mountainous landscape is reddish-brown for a brief moment, then full darkness expands. This night in early April, Grand Canyon Park and all the trimmings are no more than a flock of electrical bulbs flashing amid the conifers. Cars and trailers are moving erratically through the gigantic spider web of the side roads.

Chance brings me right in front of Mather Amphitheatre. This kind of place is usually well-heated, thanks to taxpayers' money! Its calorific potential makes it attractive. I open the massive door in time for a conference stuffed with color slides. *Shrines of all Ages*. The flat tones of voice and conventional jokes of the middle-aged people dressed in tall Boy Scout uniforms remind me of the kind of boring dope I have heard, stoically devoured by mosquitos, outdoors, from coast to coast. The very moment the lights are shut off, you find a satisfied man happily dozing, flopped down in his seat. Japanese, Australians, Italians, Yankees and Southerners. Polite applause of the cosmopolitan audience wakes me. Fraudulent parking in the back of a large hotel.

Amen. And that does it for my first day at the famous nature's shrine.

Ten o'clock the next day. High sun shining. Both elbows resting on an overhanging rail bordering the top of the cliffs. I am lazily admiring the whole of the landscape. Quite a view . . . Hundreds and hundreds of human ants — filled with pancakes, sausages, bacon, potatoes, toasts, granola, jam, marmalade, eggs, orange juice, coffee, tea, postum, vitamin and digestive pills — are moving down the trails with the goal of touching, maybe, the swift brownish holy waters of the Colorado River. Why not? Get a trail map in a jiffy, fill the water gourd, grab my torn backpack, and there I am, one more ant, accelerating on Bright Angel Trail.

Hesitant, amused, sweating, concentrated — 'focused', they say — stressed, over-confident, jubilant. There are all kinds of people expressing all kinds of feelings. At most of the elbows in the trail, and there are many, the sportive pilgrims are resting, taking snapshots, drinking water from gourds, chatting and even smoking. At one of those sharp elbows, a young couple stands quietly. Jill and Tom Agrifoglio from Hastings, Nebraska, are taking a break. Warm and communicative people. On their way down. We form a triad right away, and off we go. In spite of many severe warning posters stressing the 'excellent physical condition' needed to walk in Grand Canyon Park, we gather among many people at Indian Garden, the lunch target.

Thin, plumpish, bulky, elegant features, all shapes and all ages resting and eating there. And that, following four or five hours of steady 'breaking' along the rocky slopes of the canyon. Well-fed and now relaxed, I am looking all around when I see Jill. Even if the light April air is far from the summertime furnace down here, she is exhausted, she has really had it! While she sleeps, Tom and I walk along a rocky trail leading to Plateau Point. Colorado is down there, one thousand and two hundred feet below. The sad story comes later.

Back at Indian Garden, I realize that Jill had not recuperated much. I am not even sure that Tom can be considered at the level of the 'excellent physical condition' required to stroll down here. Climbing quickly becomes a Holy Friday calvary for them both. Very slow pace, many stops, feet sore. But I am impatient. I don't like to mark time and eye with envy the people passing us one after another. The temptation to flee from them soon takes form.

The agreeable features of two quite attractive girls climbing at high speed suddenly appears just under us. Within a few seconds they are at our side. We all walk together for five, maybe ten minutes, then a triad detaches itself from the quintet. Those hares are the two girls and myself, of course. We wait for Jill and Tom from time to time, at first. When we make such halts, I hypocritically bawl many words of encouragement to them. I am using the best words that I know, but I don't return to really help them. Our 'waiting stations' become more and more sparse. Finally, we just forget about Jill and Tom and speed up, climbing at our own pace.

Our arrival at the summit is well-timed for twilight. Members of triad number two of the memorable day are served a Scotch on the rocks in a Dodge van lit by an oil lantern shaped like in the old days but imported from Taiwan. The two attractive girls with agreeable features leave the van right after the drink. I leave the van too, leave its coldness and darkness. Can't stand it. Mild music — guitar and violin — played by good musicians at the Blue Angel Lounge would be better for my body and my soul. Savor some Grand Marnier. Stare at Arizona's wild mountains darkened by the long night, through a window. Shall be on the road anew, in the morning.

To you all, people who have read my work, please forgive me for not having succeeded very much in describing how dirty I have been towards Jill and Tom. Too excited, blinded by the girls. A good occasion to lend a hand traded for a sterile sportive exploit with two nurses. One working 'intensive care', the other one, 'psychiatric', in a large hospital. Closing hour of the bar. Somebody help me out. Tomorrow will surely be another day.

Sartre's Shadow
over Chicago

My first and only visit to Chicago was a complete disaster. Gray Sunday morning, late April 1980. Cold raging rain coming from Lake Michigan. I entered the city on Freeway 55. Just as if the tides of geological thrusts had risen high in turmoil, quieted down, eroded, and risen again, the whole process moved to the point where there remained nothing but a peneplain encrusted with debris — railroad tracks, half demolished red brick factories, burst oil tanks, rotten steel structures — of each of the industrial periods which, at the same time, gave a sense, fed and shook the great conurbation, the whole, still full of life with new features stemming here and there from the surface of the man-made urban landscape.

That goes for the entry. Noon found me shivering and crouched in the van parked just beside Burnham Park, corner of 31st, a bowl of hot soup in hand. Before I left southern California, a little earlier in the spring, an architect friend born in Chicago marked and encircled two large areas of a city map of his hometown.

'These are the black slum areas. Never go there, day or night. You might easily get killed.' Today, quite irresponsibly, I know that I will pick one of these two areas for a ride. Daytime at least. The hot zone privileged as a magnet for my random trip expands just northwest of the handful of prestigious old and new skyscrapers clustered on the waterfront.

This ready-to-be-lived scenario reminds me of something similar that I experienced in Philadelphia many years ago. That was nothing but a short incursion in a one hundred per cent black area expanding just east of Temple University. No car that time. Pedestrian. Vulnerable. Had to cross two half-demolished, half-abandoned streets, with all the purposefulness of a sanitary cordon, before hitting a living area beginning with the third one. Black kids, black middle-aged people, black elderly people, black streetcar conductors, black merchants. From my hiding place it seemed that even the cats were black!

Today, in Chicago, I find not only a few streets in miserable condition, but everywhere I drive, and everywhere I can see, to each side and in front, the whole black area expresses painfully the crude feeling of having been submitted to an overly long aging process — accelerated, in many places, by successful and triumphant demolition. Groups of people of all ages, but mostly tense young adults are clustered on street corners.

'What the hell are they waiting for, all these Godots!' I exclaim. Many people stare at the van in a dry manner. Of course, it must be said that, with its fancy metallic two-tone dorado paint, its large white shiny bumpers and chromed wheel centers, my van looks quite good. Stiff neck. Soon, become too anxious to stop at the traffic lights. Frantically burn the red ones. Speed up towards the prestigious area, only a few blocks away. On time for the oncoming fog of twilight.

Wrigley and Playboy Buildings, Tribune Tower, a couple of museum facades, two or three massive sculptures and so on; the first part of the afternoon had been filled with a quite conventional tour of Michigan Avenue and the waterfront near Chicago River. On a few occasions, while strolling, some well-intentioned passers-by gave me the tip not to miss Marshall & Fields, a famous department store. It is quite a beautiful one, I have to admit. Good taste, interesting design, sumptuous, and . . . warm inside. Dancing on fragile high-heeled shoes (fixed on their feet with tiny straps), dressed-up ladies completely ignored the cold weather while walking gracefully on the wet sidewalks before entering the store. That was so crazy. That was so charming.

Books and newspapers from France were being sold at one spot on the third or fourth floor. Bought a copy of *Le Monde*. Picked up the news inside that Jean-Paul Sartre, the philosopher, had died on the fifteenth of the month. Also bought a copy of the *Sunday Sun-Times*. A wise guy in charge of the column on architecture had searched and found somewhere that the French philosopher had come here on a journalist's tour, in 1945. 'Sartre's view of American Life.' In that short piece, I found nothing but ruthless and harsh things written about American cities. I don't like it when someone, whether local product or outsider, takes on the easy task of criticizing. After all, our towns are more than bunches of problems, aren't they? Anyway, I came close to shouting, 'That little bastard!' Yeah, I came close to shouting but I didn't, because so many of the fundamental criticisms of his harsh article were true and still are. But let's leave that hot potato aside, and put the newspapers to rest for the time being. The Chicago Odyssey has been sufficiently heavy without it. I have had enough of it all.

Feel like getting to sleep early. No doubt. Slowly climb in the van. Southbound on Shore Drive to find a quiet place for the night. Leave the Drive and try Pershing. Come back on the Drive and try 47th. Come back again and try 51st. Too crowded with cars, too well-lit, too noisy; there is something bothering me everywhere. It also seems that most of the people living on these streets, if not all, are black.

What a sin! But even if the atmosphere in many places is one of aging — a feature which is not typical of colored people's areas in Chicago! — they are not really slums.

Well-dressed people, whole families most probably coming back from eating out or visiting friends and relatives, are entering big mansions transformed into multi-apartment buildings. Yes, all that is fair and nice, but I do not feel too secure about sleeping around . . . Go back on South Drive again. I will hit the spot near Jackson Park on 57th. Confession. For a minimal amount of rest, have to swallow a somniferous pill at night.

While checking some geographic features in a road atlas the next morning — once I have dug myself out of my warm sleeping bag, I notice that the fog has disappeared. Looking around then with ingenuousness and curiosity, I find that my van had been parked beside the second black slum marked on the city map by my Chicago friend, who now lives in sunny southern California. Where's the truth, where's the legend . . .

Sunset Boulevard
and the Tramp Lady

Today I had quite a euphoric drive on Sunset Boulevard. It began in the city center of Los Angeles, then I moved out. After sightseeing colorful and very stimulating, densely populated areas, I found myself caught by twilight at the height of Beverly Hills. Energized by a strong need to see the ocean, I stuck to the wheel. From Bel Air, the last section of the drive was performed on a curved narrow road. Through the open windows of the van I noted the existence of gardens, beautiful trees, security guards and dogs, electrical fences and fine mansions screwed to the rocks on both sides of the road. But maybe I just dreamed or nightmared that last portion of the drive.

Then the open sea. Landed in a sunny spot, somewhere in Santa Monica. Was it Will Rogers Beach? Was it Topango Beach? Who the hell knows! One thing is sure. The Pacific was right there. Fair weather and lots of stars, all that free of charge. Walked along the tideline. Very light tapping of waves. It was hightide. A few steps away the beach gradually narrowed, squeezed between the ocean and Road 1 northbound for Santa Barbara. Cars, mostly small, speeded up in the dark. Intense headlights looked far away. Here, big pieces of rock, washed up by the tides, locked the beach a few yards ahead. That put an end to my hike. Dinnertime anyway. Ready to go back.

Up to that very moment had thought I was the only person on the shore but suddenly I discerned someone in the gloom. Someone was doing something I couldn't see in the very near background. I heard the clink of bottles. Walked a few yards closer. It was a woman. I would have guessed middle-aged at first glance, but who can tell for sure? With remnants of beauty, she was at the same time attractive and repulsive. One hand held a bag. Grocery store paper bag with handles. The clink still sounded from inside, where empty beer bottles mingled with a few pieces of torn clothes. I did not feel at ease. There was something wrong . . .

Courteous and urbane as I am, I started talking anyway. (Was I half-consciously searching for an easy good fortune at that very moment? Most probably. No matter. Be at ease, reader. There was none.) My instant companion took care of the biggest part of the conversation and I just let her take the lead. Had a lot of troubles here and there in southern California, with this one and that one. For many years. The closer in time, the worse it got. Hardly bearable to listen to. Now on her way north. Towards Seattle where close relatives live. Wanted to leave the shit behind. Hasn't seen her folks for many years. Expected a lot from this pilgrimage to her childhood country. Hitchhiking in daylight, and so on.

She went on for a while, but the conversation gradually became less and less 'good'. Whatever the subject, the lady became more and more aggressive, nervous, paranoid. Maybe it was the effect of the darkness, maybe she was fed up, I don't know. One thing is for sure. Just couldn't stand it any longer! I got up — we had been seated on the sand — and looked straight into her face. What I saw was the skin peeled off a wild animal ready to jump forward, to scream, to run away. A tense mix of all of these things. I wondered what she saw on my own face?

Both of us quickly managed to find a way to leave the hot spot. No exchange of names, no more exchange of anything. She irritably picked up her paper bag. The clinking started again. The sound decreased this time, as she walked slowly on the thick sand. A bar appeared on the civilized side of Road Number 1. Kind of road stop garnished with crude lighting fixtures. That's where she went. Absolutely had to drag a guy, anyone, to get food, drink, bed. Her poor merchandisable and sullied body, her humiliated soul.

I walked straight to the van. Lit up the oil

lamp. Opened a bottle of wine and threw the cork far away among shells and rocks. I could still hear the sandpipers roaming amidst the yellowish foam pushed away by the tide. Absent-mindedly, splashed a full can of *chili con carne* in the pan, then sat on the side step. Felt relieved that the tramp lady walked away, but the brief encounter left a sour taste in my mouth. Ruminated about the kind of personal pedigree that she lay bare on the beach. Ruminated so much around these things that I found my dinner feast half burnt in the pan.

Not much use trying to disentangle anything tonight. Better leave to you, reader, the plain facts. No vicious literary essay building up the tramp lady's sufferings, now or later. Just expressing the painful encounter is fair and honest. Cleaning dishes and coming back to the side step. Too late to go anywhere this evening. The glare of the neon lights of the bar keep on flashing by the road side. The small cars speed up, heading for Santa Barbara or any other spot beyond Santa Monica. Close the van doors. Blow out the oil lamp. A full day, and Sunset Boulevard is far away.

Hot Teepee at Dark

'Where the hell are we going, Joe?'

Driving up and down rolling hills in the dark, turning here and there, I've had about enough of the Coney Island roller-coaster style drive. That's why I shout loudly to my fellow companion. Quiet smile but not a single word, passenger side . . . Joe Servais, of French and Indian blood, is no doubt wiser than I am. Tonight at least. Anyway, no more than half an hour after my verbal explosion, we arrive at our destination point. Somewhere in the back hills of Poway and Escondido, close to the Mexican border. The Dodge van gets stuck in the mud of the steep driveway. A thin row of lights shines in the cool night. Dogs bark in the heavy way they bark anywhere on earth where there is an Indian encampment.

Tonight, the encampment is a mobile home. But we don't step inside. Instead, two or three people pop out as they pass by the front door and join us on our way up the steep hill. Short of breath a little. On a small plateau cleaned out among the rocks stands a small round tent. Campfire crackles and shoots flames high in the icy air. A curing ceremony will be held here for the benefit of a person seriously ill. She is now lying in a hospital. The ceremony takes place in what the Indians call a sweat lodge.

Bomer is handy. He has worked well. The floor of the plateau has been swept clean of even the smallest branch of wood and of the most microscopic pebble. Piles of black volcanic stones, mixed with the ambers, are turning red. Small branches of black sage are lying by the tent's entrance in such a way that everyone can pick up a couple on the way inside. The wait is not long. Jim Quizquiz tells us shortly: 'Time to go in.' Jackets, sweaters, shirts, pants, dresses, underwear, shoes, boots and socks off; the whole place is silent now, everyone undresses.

As 'sweat leader', Jim bends and crawls inside first. They follow him, one by one, Ramon and Virginia Balardes, both of whom are about sixty years of age, Julia, the niece or daughter of the former, Joe Servais, the guy from Valley Center who invited me to come here, a couple more people, Olga and Mona, I think, then myself. Seven dark hot stones already warm up the place. The 'doorman', that is Bomer, is asked by Jim to carefully close the door cloth so to keep the heat inside. Sage branches are dipped in a bucket, and water is sprinkled over the rocks. Steam quickly fills the tent. We are physically very close to one another. Bodies begin to sweat.

Soon, the sweat leader calls for a general invocation and for the presence of Godfather among us. He also speaks about the sick lady lying on a hospital bed. Then, one by one, we say a few words about the same. All our energies are brought together. Silent night. We hear Bomer working with care, outside, to keep the fire strong over the remaining hot stones. He is soon called by the sweat leader. Bomer knows what it means. The tent door is opened from the outside. Seven more volcanic stones, now glowing red, are ceremoniously presented to Jim. The stones are set in a row pattern oriented towards a hole dug in the center of the tent, already filled with the seven previous ones. When the stones are arranged all together, the door is closed again. Darkness comes back inside. A generous sprinkle of water generates a burst of hot steam.

I do feel good with all of this. We go for another circle of invocations, chants, and prayers, the entrance of the stones being repeated three more times during the ceremony, to make a total of twenty-eight. A number which has a religious meaning, a meaning already forgotten. At one point in one of the circles, Jim asks each one of us, clockwise and starting from his left, to express our own personal feelings towards Godfather. Everyone proceeds with dignity. Everyone is meditative. I didn't know Indians could express themselves with such a lack of ego, of pride, with such ingenuousness. I didn't know Indians could cry with such warm tears.

When my turn comes to speak to Godfather, I feel at first painfully stuck and filled with displaced 'common decency' and ridiculous 'self-respect'. But I don't remain mute for long. Finally focus on my youngest daughter and my youngest son, both about eighteen and living at the far north-east end of the continent. They have a troubled life at the time. Be satisfied reader, I have had my own turn at crying anyways . . . Well, Ramon, Virginia, Julia and so on, we all go quite far, dealing with the self-involving circle.

It seems quite late when the ceremony is over and we crawl outside. The stars are shining with something cruel, only mineral impassiveness maybe, from the dark velvet of the Californian night. It is so cold that I even refuse the usually welcome bucket of water over my head as I go out. Everyone dresses. Later, instant coffee and cookies are swallowed in the mobile home which we are allowed to enter this time. All that mixed with a lot of talking. While chewing a biscuit, I wonder how Godfather will react to our sweating ceremony. Will he cure the sick lady, at least?

The Skunks
and the Cardinals

Early in November and westbound for the Pacific. I was in search of a bunch of genuine bohemian friends travelling in a decrepit red and white bakery truck topped with tarpaulins and oversized teepee poles. The whole thing looked like a shaking bazaar matchbox. Even if afflicted with poor sight, you just couldn't miss such an antique. But, at the same time, how could two mobile vehicles moving freely in the open spaces of America, whatever their recognizable features, set a position in which to meet? Nonsense!

That was in Arizona. Some veteran hippies I had met at Indian Healing Waters informed me that the travelling bohemians might be strolling around Ashram Akasha, on the river-bank of San Pedro River, twenty-four miles north of Benson. A river? Ha! Thin trickles of water on a very wide, dry, sandy bed flanked with high, steep, bushy banks. Driving on a dirt road as curved as a drunk snake, I finally found the spot around mid-afternoon of a very fine, sunny day.

I say 'finally' because, blindly driven towards a record number of dead ends by a cheap screwed-on dashboard compass which had gone out of business, I had lost my way some time ago. So, wisely forgetting about the crazy magnetic needle, I decided to follow road signs, even the small ones, half torn out, half obliterated, which, on fourth-class roads, are always the most useful. As I mentioned above, I eventually arrived at Ashram Akasha. There weren't many people there at that time of the year. Were there many more at any other season? I don't know.

Anyway, the ones that I met, and the encounter didn't take place much before the evening, were a bunch of heteroclite personages in the real theatrical sense, and very good people as well. Most of their faces have faded away since, but I do remember a young German boy who left our company late at night with the firm idea of sleeping in the desert. There wasn't far to go! Backpack, water gourd, high boots, bell to chase rattlesnakes: the guy was equipped with the full paraphernalia and was ready for an exotic initiation. The initiation of a European kid to the Arabian nights of our open spaces.

Let's go back now to the afternoon of that sunny day in November. It's four o'clock. A battered and dusty station wagon full of all sorts of stuff turned painfully in the yard and came to a halt with a moan. A very tall, bearded, open-faced man in his early forties stepped out of the vehicle. Soul, spirit, and 'man of the place', he was simply known as Ivan. In spite of the clear fact that he drove a modern piece of noisy and stinky machinery still steaming and rattling, the tall bearded man came straight out — according to my on-the-spot fantasy — of a storybook. A book telling about ancient times. My vision was one of a biblical patriarch walking with a majestic air on loose gravel. In spite of the passing of a squadron of military jet planes — striping the blue sky with cotton, fan-shaped tails — the vivid flashback kept me in Palestine, Jordan, and other similar sacred lands.

Later in the day, after a solitary dinner, I met all the people in the main house of Ashram. Most of the voices were a little high-pitched when I dropped in. A little too high for sure. Some voices were even acrimonious. A diversion was expected. The diversion came in the person of Ivan, my biblical patriarch. Stomping on the floor with a long wooden stick, he improvised a parodic declamation, a humoristic parable. People had no choice but to laugh or, at least, to smile. Full face. Harmony came back to the big wooden house. Thanks be to God! I do hate troubles.

One of the former tempestuous chorists was a young woman. Pregnant. Only a few more months to go. Her poor body afflicted with a skin disease. Suffering an almost-permanent burning, itching. Had tried all kinds of doctors and medicines. No success. Difficult to sleep, difficult to relax. At first, she made me nervous, stiff and reluctant. Then I looked at her straight in the eyes. They were frightened like a deer's and expressed such an open gentleness. The whole thing gradually awoke in me, a so-called 'tough guy', what some connoisseurs of words would label compassion.

All right. You all know the way I felt and how I melted in the situation, but let's cut it short. As a road runner, there is no use letting myself slip on the soft sides of my own macadam. Anyway, whatever be the peculiar psychical and physical features of the people gathered that evening on the floor of Ashram's main house, the time came to go back to the van for some sleep. When I refused the invitation to stay in that warm house and went outside, I didn't know that a very low temperature would be registered during the night. I certainly didn't know that the big brown box on wheels would become a well-running and powerful refrigerator to freeze me to the marrow of my bones during the night.

I woke up shivering at dawn. As I started to walk on the cold sand, luckily enough, a totally unforeseen image popped up on my mental screen and began to warm me up . . . While strolling among the conifers flanking the banks of the San Pedro River, at sunset, the day before, a whole family of skunks had come close to me, in a very familiar way, even frolicking between my legs. While I stood still with those playmates nearby — do I have to say why? — exactly twelve cardinals springing from the sky suddenly started (I know that you will find it hard to believe) dancing a ballet around me. Then, just as if obeying an invisible signal expressed by a mysterious and benevolent elf, they all clustered on a small bush. Red shot, a sun racing towards the horizon line, set them ablaze.

I am pretty sure now that the skunks, the birds and all the innocent animals living around the Ashram were planning on doing something good in the near future for the poor girl in an advanced state of pregnancy, for her almost-permanent painful itching. I do believe that. Well, the story is over. Oh yes! About the German kid living his own Arabian night in the Arizona desert? Never saw him come back. Never saw him again. Maybe the whole situation was in need of a propitiatory victim. But who can tell for certain.

Sunrise and Sunset
with Luna

San Francisco is my beloved Pacific town, and
Luna Moth, the first person that I met there.
Friends of friends not seen for long, wrong
family name given, the odds were really against
any potential encounter. Communication channel was miraculously linked and we made it.
Our very first meeting took place in a deluxe
vegetarian restaurant. We ate something between a late breakfast and an early lunch. The
weather was pitiful that Saturday morning in
late November. I felt sad and a little depressed.

'When it is rainy and foggy in San Francisco
we feel like we are in a gray pearl,' Luna said
amidst servings of green salad, hot pie, choco-
late cake and exotic fruits. Her way of inter-
preting the weather put everything back in its
place.

Radio broadcast was not better for Sunday,
but we travelled to the country anyway. Was it
in the Santa Cruz mountains, Santa Clara valley
or the very first hills of the Diabolo Range?
Pardon me Californians, my memory is weak
today. The continuation of the story should

give you a few tips about its geographical setting. If you find were I was, please let me know. One basic fact is indisputable. We travelled really deep in the forest. Luna Moth had a trailer stranded along a muddy dirt road, halfway down a gully.

Quiet, peaceful Mathusalem, one of the main targets of our country visit, was standing not too far away. Mathusalem is more than two thousand years old. Mathusalem is a sequoia. Had never seen a giant redwood before. Couldn't guess I was seeing a tree either. Its substance was something between stone and metal-like material. Absolutely nothing related to wood in structure or in appearance. Sculptured by the combined action of time and of inclement weather, and, if not enough, struck and set afire more than once by powerful shots of lighting, it appeared much closer to a geological phenomenon than to any vegetal species.

So wide, so tall. Had almost to break my neck to see leaves and 'true' living branches topping the whole monument. But there were many! Nearby, a companion of Mathusalem was quite as big and as impressive. Both of them brought me back to my own human scale in space and time. Even a crow may live as long as a man, if not longer. What about those sequoias with all their years of life behind them?

My pride quickly deflated in front of those

long-living sturdy fellows, for who was I? Probably nothing more than a passing feather, a dressed and talkative ant. Also, the terrible dampness of the woods was depressing me again, from chin to heels. Fortunately, we didn't stay there too long. Helpful Luna, fairy Luna took me almost by the hand on another hike, short compared to that first one. This time, towards a rustic cabin perched among and over rocks and trees. There were some odd fellows there. But I didn't even give them a glance and walked straight inside the cabin.

A young friend of Luna, who had Russian ancestors and looked like a beautiful wild flower, lived there. The girl, I was told later, acted and was recognized as a first class belly dancer in Frisco's nightclubs. She didn't perform at home on that rainy day in November, but we were offered some hot home-baked cake straight out of the oven, along with steaming coffee and European liquor, a generous treat. I was no longer feeling like a passing feather, and my ego inflated again to attain its normal convenient shape.

Then we drove back to town. Luna seemed to know everybody and everything in town. My social network built up. One day, speaking about this and that, the conversation focused on earthquakes, a permanent, red-hot subject for those who live near the active San Andreas fault. Nuclear war was a similarly non-frolicking topic. My optimistic temper has a rough time dealing with the apocalyptical terrestrial circus in general, 'the bomb' in particular. I was seriously stressed again when Luna spoke up. And what she said had the virtue of a parable. A wise and gentle one. I felt better, I smiled again. The approximate words follow: 'Ten years ago, some friends had domestic cement shelters built at high cost to protect themselves against the eventuality of an atomic bomb. At the same time, other friends planted fruit trees. Today, crevices run along the walls of the shelters whereas the trees have already borne fruit.'

At the time I met her, Luna was living on Douglas street, a very steep one. But she didn't live in her house. The place was rented to close friends. She lived behind. A small shack. Crowded with all sorts of things. Nicely decorated with her own drawings. Driving her Volvo car, she went every morning towards the summit of one of the numerous hills of San Francisco, trademark of my beloved Pacific town. Right on time for sunrise. She again jumped in her vehicle late every afternoon. This time to contemplate the sunset. Every day, Luna created a small watercolor painting about her vision of the sun. Last year I received one of those paintings in the mail. It was circular-shaped and filled with blue, gray and orange. I am still not sure if it was a sunset or a sunrise.

Shrimp Fishing
in Good Company

While following Road 82 in Louisiana, along-side the Gulf of Mexico, I crossed Sabine Pass, the road number became 87, I was landing in Texas. But I didn't go far among the six-gallon hat people on that sunny and windy day of November 1979. The Dodge van was to loaf a full day and a full night, right on the Texan side of a bridge expanding over Sabine Pass. And between the Pass and the Sabine River, there is Lake Calcasieu. They say 'lake' but this geographical feature is filled with salt water. No, I didn't burn up much road that day in November because Bart, a young fisherman, had a first-class hangover.

He owned a boat, but not a single tool at hand to fix its small outboard motor. An engine not at all willing to perform its duty and push a peewee-sized aluminum boat straight towards a fishing area somewhere in the marshes. Somewhere far inland on Lake Calcasieu. So, the young fisherman had no repair outfit at hand, but two steel boxes full of tools were lying in my van. Pliers, wrench, screwdriver, and so forth, pulled out in a jiffy from my treasure chests. There was not much mechanical trouble and he adjusted the motor quickly.

'What about some shrimp fishing? Why don't you come in? I'll bring you back later.'

Standing in the aluminum boat, now afloat, the young fisherman was in a hurry and a bit impatient. Didn't give me a minute to think and — thanks to him! — I had secured a beautiful day.

First, a few sparse explosions. Second, many more. Third, blue smoke and a steady shrill noise. Shifted into gear. Then full speed over the choppy waters of the lake. I say 'over' because we were soaring! Every time the bottom hit one of those waves, it was just like landing on a mountain slope filled with rocks. Quickly became anxious about the near future of my bones and features. Yes, I had to take care to stick to my seat with a firm grip, or get out. And fast.

When we arrived at the fisherman-who-had-a-hangover's shack, I felt that, with all the tom-tom over the short waves, most of my ribs were broken. The lake drive had also given me a kind of heavy drinking hangover effect, but it didn't last for long. As soon as the engine had been cut off, I began to feel the place, to be immersed in the whole flat landscape. The plain beauty of the marshes in the autumn. A moving feast emphasized by the beach, crowned with low-flying sea birds and shore birds, the quivering blue waters. Everything had a taste of the infinite . . . All that neutralizing of time, too many days lived with both hands gripped on the steering wheel.

Bert's shack was erected above the waterline, but not too far. Shaking gangway and platform extended over the lake, nearby. We had company there! Two jolly good fellows, one slim, one plump, were standing on the old planks. Cleaning and sorting huge piles of shrimps splashed on a low counter, Paw Paw and F.D. were at work (F for Faxton and D for something I forget). Fishing had been good during the last few days, and much more than a couple of buckets of shrimps were in line, all ready to be cleaned and washed.

Two or three hours of outdoor light work went by quickly. We ate a bit in the shack. Slices of white bread, baloney, mustard, a can of beer. Back on duty soon after. More sun, more wind, more shrimps cleaned. Fishing net's visiting hours came fast. Three musketeers plus one, quite a merry team, went aboard at a quick pace. Horse riding in the peewee-sized aluminum boat and over the waves. Do not know at all if I brought good luck on that sunny and windy day in November, but the record catch in the life of those fishermen was right there: three hundred pounds of shrimps — one shot, one net — mixed with crabs of all sizes, catfish and a couple of superb flounders. The yelling was loud.

The whole bunch of seafood, carefully twisted in the net, came into sight alongside the raft, the big ball dripping from everywhere. Much less work making a shrimp's ball with a net than trying to lift the whole thing over the raft! With their feet skidding on the half-submerged platform, the merry team performed a wild ballet. Rubber boots or not, everyone had to move quickly around the primitive winch's screwed-on frame. At one point during the shrimp-salvaging-and-rescuing operation, Bart jumped straight into the lake. Pushing the heavy hard ball from under, he made the difference between failure and success, he became a sub-aquatic hero.

Screaming, swearing, we succeeded. No time to lose after that. Sun goes down fast in the fall. First move. The hauling gang was brought back to the gangway. Second move, and last one for me today. A fast ride back to Cameron, the place where the journey had found its seeds. Phone call to Benton, fisherman's father. In Sulphur, just north of Lake Calcasieu. Freshness equaling value, the shrimps had to be sold quickly or frozen. Brief loading on the shore. Sudden chill in the neck. Sudden chill in the whole body. Quite cool at night in southern Louisiana when the sun goes down and the wind still blows.

Warming up inside the van. Light, cracking

noise outside. It was the wind, playing from time to time on the truck's body. Short waiting period. Strong headlights of a vehicle suddenly lit up the whole place. Spinning of wheels on soft sand. Then the quiet sound of a motor turning idle. Disappearance of the lights. Door slamming. A tall and energetic fellow, topped with a mechanic's cap, moved forward out of the shadow. He came into sight. It was Benton. First-class coffee steaming in the pot. No cream but smooth Scotch as a substitute. Oil lamp smelling. That's an aroma I like. We felt good inside but there wasn't much time for chatting. Swiftly swallowing the 'hot drug', Benton expressed a warm invitation to spend the next weekend here.

'I will show you birds, aquatic life, everything.'

And he left, running over the waves. In the dark. Me? Totally out of business.

Deep sleep. Stone-like. A snoring stone. Later at night, someone knocked lightly on the side of the van. Opened one eye. Opened the side door. Strong, good smell of sea products invaded the place. A bucket held by hands, a bucket more than half full of shrimps, Benton was standing there.

'That's your share of the sea crop for today's work.'

Lots of perishable food for a lonely ranger, I thought to myself. I said yes to that valuable gift, but resisted eighteen bucks to complement the salary paid by nature. No way to argue with Benton. To take money and shrimps both corresponded with his idea of fairness. I went back to sleep.

On my way to Galveston, the next day, most of the shrimps were given — pardon me, Benton . . . pardon me, Bart — to a few people along the road. There were many *why*'s explaining that free-of-charge distribution but telling the *why* would mean building up a whole new story. So let's forget about it. The money? Secured under the driver's seat, and there was no problem of freshness keeping it there. It was also to be given. To a single person this time. A hitchhiker going back home to the West Coast, who, I am sure, did well with those few bucks as he was quite broke.

And that's the shrimp fishing story. The ending is a bit flat, I know. To tell the truth, my real intent was to talk more about those fine people I met on Lake Calcasieu. It seems clear now that the damn shrimps squeezed all the juice out of the writing because they wanted to be in the limelight. The hell with them, I say, I missed my point, but one day, when I am less crazy on the road, more reasonable, I shall take some leisure time, go back around southern Louisiana, and write a story dealing more with the good human company.

By the time I become 'less crazy on the road, more reasonable', Bart will have begun driving the powerful fishing boat that he spoke to me about, between two mouthfuls, during lunchtime back at the shack. And, by then, I am seriously afraid that Benton, Bart, and this writer will have attained an age that many will consider respectable.

Clanking Noise
of Slot Machines
on the Strip

Around five in the afternoon, I was rolling slowly on the Strip when a promotion agent for Nevada's famous Fun Capital of the World passed me a whole bunch of tabloid-sized newspapers through the van window.

'All this is free,' said the guy with a professional shark smile.

I parked the Dodge vehicle alongside the sidewalk in a jiffy and made a brief inventory of the documentation. It was mainly magazines and news for adults. Water soon filled my mouth, my ears began to twinge and my eyes to twinkle.

According to the *Mirror Gazette*, every girl in town was asking me to phone her: Mistress Lena, to put me in my place; Lila, to be taught to be a whole woman; Crystal, a former air stewardess, to fly with; Roseanne, to show me the time of my life; Traci, to give me what she's got; Mona Lisa, to be my slave; Yvette, to make my fantasies come true . . . I finally decided to

call a fresh twenty-year-old woman who promised to let a breath of spring into my life.

Controlling my impatience to speak directly
to such a marvel, but still brandishing and
waving the pink-and-black tabloid, I walked
towards a public phone booth and dialed.

'Hello, is Key there?'

'Who?'

'Key . . .'

'Wait . . .' Then followed all the rattle
made by a busy switchboard operator at the
peak hour of the day.

'She's out!' Out for lunch, for a dentist's
appointment, out of business, the answering
matron didn't say . . .

'How much will it be if she comes back?'

'Seventy-five dollars in cash. By the way,
where is your hotel?'

'No hotel, but . . .'

'Rent a room first!' Clang.

A little abashed, a little angry, I went back
to my van and started rolling again, along the
Strip. The pink-and-black *Mirror Gazette* was
on the passenger's seat. The wind turned the
pages. It was now open at the middle. Right
over the announcements of Seductive Playmates and Enchanted Beauties, covering half
the page, John McCarthy, Sheriff of Las Vegas
& Clark County, was also announcing something encircled by a pair of handcuffs. Speaking
off the cuff, Sheriff McCarthy was saying, 'To
solicit or accept services from a prostitute

could result in your arrest. Do not ruin your vacation by going to jail.'

I became pale, then said *in petto*, 'Maybe I was close to experiencing some trouble.' But what about Lena, Lila, Crystal, Roseanne, Traci, Yvette and Key? If they were pussy cats, they were surely also wild cats, able to play their phone games without being molested by the cops. Maybe their telephone kit was located somewhere outside of Las Vegas & Clark County. But how then could they all promise to be in any room within fifteen, twenty or thirty minutes? Did they take advantage of a helicopter service? At that point in my investigation, bored and disillusioned, I refused to go any further in the process of deduction. I made a mental note to send the entire stuff to 13 Baker Street, London.

Anyway, the van's carburetor flooded at that very moment. Right in front of the Palomino. And Palomino is the right place to appreciate a first-class striptease. Each and every girl is a real professional artist: sense of rhythm, witty, elegant, well-mannered. Took a first-class seat to attend the first-class show. There was only one inch between my red nose and the stage. When a stripper came close, I instinctively tried to move my seat back. But it wouldn't budge. I blushed and looked a little to the side of the high-heeled shoes dancing close by.

If there had been only that! At one point in the show, the audience's clap-clap and yelling became louder than ever. The star of stars, Joy, was stepping on the stage. But Joy was apparently facing some technical difficulties in undoing the clasp of her bra. With disarming ingenuity, she came straight over to me, bent, turned, and asked with a smile if I would give her a helping hand. The helping hand was really shaking and I was not seeing things too well. Do not remember how I succeeded with the rebel clasp. Perhaps I just broke it by sheer accident. Not much later, the gorilla bodyguard working for the Palomino told me straight out that if I did not buy any more drinks, I would have to move out. I moved out.

Night had come to Las Vegas. Parked on the wrong side of Freemont Street, eyes half closed, I was smoking a cheap cigar. Joy was dancing lasciviously on the big blue puffs of smoke when, framed by the van's window just like a western actress on the TV screen, a spicy cowgirl suddenly appeared. But the cowgirl was not an actress. She was an official personnage, she was a traffic agent on foot.

'You are parked in a no-parking area, sir. Here is your ticket.'

She hit me twice on the shoulder with the two-buck ticket, then was gone. I would have paid twenty-five dollars to see her again but she was already lost between the moving cars.

And Joy was no longer dancing on the big blue puffs of my cheap cigar.

Turned on the ignition key, put the head-lights on, and went rolling again on the Strip. A Niagara of lights. Caesar's Palace, Golden Nugget, Horseshoe, Four Queens, Flamingo, Aladdin, Tropicana, Stardust, Silver Slipper. Hotels, casinos, bars, restaurants, all their lights were brightly flashing. Little Chapel of the Flowers was offering complete wedding services 24 hours a day, while Monterey Hotel, among others, was advertising full-length X-rated movies plus 'love machines' (limited quantity) right in the room. Tahiti, Casa Malaga and Tivoli Motels were advertising up to five hard-core films served in water beds sur-rounded by mirrored walls and ceilings. Old-style burlesque, music hall revues, acrobatic dancers, the Strip was also featuring the best shows in the world, not to mention the deli-cacies of its fine cuisine.

One, two, three, I drew a deep, long breath then walked straight towards the main en-trance of one of the biggest and most famous casinos in Las Vegas. Dozing like rag puppets with a dash of drool in the corner of their mouths, were crippled people seated in rolling chairs, driven around by sexy, attractive girls. Dressed in more-or-less clean robes, inflated by big Maroccan leather wallets full of petrol dollars, their Arabic-styled head topped with comic turbans, some strange people spoke an incomprehensible gibberish while a small black goatee went up and down in rhythm with the motion of their mouths.

Reverends, pastors, monsignors, brothers, priests, and more of the same kind, strolled around, concealed in conventional lay suits, or Hawaiian shirts coupled with oversized, ridiculous Bermudas. Showing small, medium or big tits, walking light or heavy on low, medium, or high heels, young, middle-aged and over-middle-aged whores turned their permanently smiling heads in slow motion. The electric candelabras fixed on the low ceilings enlightening their well-combed blonde, black, brown, red or platinum hair. Yellow Chinese, black Africans, red-brown Latin Americans, flour-white Europeans, mainly tomato-red or copper-tanned North Americans, displayed all the skin colors imaginable but the same obsessed eyes, full of lust.

Wealthy, just-arrived people and toast-and-jam people, unable to afford much more than the nickle-and-dime slot machines, circulated from room to room. Side by side with the pocket-eyed faces of the elderly they walked among the angel faces of the young in despair. Professional poker-head gamblers searched for fat fishes, money-minded wise girls escorted all kinds of scraps, abnormals rolling dirty red balls in pale faces, plain stealers, opium, cocaine, speed, hashish, and other drug addicts, heavy criminals quickly spending the easy bucks, sadistic characters, congressmen, born-to-be victims, mafioso cousins, and so on. In this casino, as in any casino in Las Vegas, the busy wild fauna had the look and the aroma of the famous French *Cour des Miracles*.

Baccarat, blackjack, roulette, craps, keno, how did I spend my fortune that night? With a single twenty-dollar bill rolled and secured in my eyeglass case, it was pure fantasy, but the mood perfectly appropriate. One crowded room featured *chemin de fer*, which is baccarat. Stentorian voice, bald head, piggy red eyes, a thirty-five-year old personage, straight out of Hunter S. Thomson's *Fear and Loathing in Las Vegas*, was scratching a match on his thigh to light his fourth enormous, stinky cigar, just beside delicate ladies dressed in lace and covered with jewels.

Triumphant, cruel, the unmannered fellow threw cards and chips as if he was firing bullets. He swept off everything. The other players, silent, had faces like mourners. At one point in the railroad game, the croupier, a European, didn't even succeed in shuffling the cards. They all flew around the 'shoe'. The poor man had to be escorted out of the room. Another croupier, also a European, swiftly replaced him. Long, pale, thin, tight-lipped, four or five members of the personnel wearing black suits paced the bacarrat room, like old crows flying low over decaying carcasses spotted in hay fields.

After a filling two-buck meal swallowed in a remote, dark area of the casino, I returned towards the playground area. Cling-clang of the slot machines here and there, loud burst of laughter, disco music, high-pitched voices of hysterical eighty-year-old ladies acting as if they were eighteen, rattle of the little white ball in the fast-turning roulette, echoes of bottles and glasses clinking in the bars, the stern voice of a croupier saying, '*Rien ne va plus.*' The sound-film was perfectly okay.

Nevertheless, a dash of fresh air was an urgent need. I looked around to spot the casino exit. Couldn't find the damned door! A Machiavellian trick played by rows of mirrors and a circular room design drove me to turn and return to the playground area. I soon percieved myself as a third-class Theseus wandering in a labyrinth where the croupiers were Minotaur's creatures and symbols. And when I saw the security guards posted at every strategic corner, I admitted that my chances of escaping were thin.

A buxom blonde security girl, with an enormous six-shooter balanced alongside her big thigh, suddenly came straight towards me. This night was heading for a tragic ending, I realized then, not cool at all. At the very same moment I saw a door and ran for it. Crash! The door was a mirage, another mirror.

When I woke up I was leaning against a stinky garbage bin in the backyard of the casino. The night air was pure. The stars shone brightly. I had a bump as big as a lemon on the left side of my head and my eyeglass case was in my right hand. I opened it. The twenty dollar bill was still fortunately rolled up inside. When I closed the case, I distinctly heard a mockingbird flying by and laugh: 'Ha! Ha! Ha!'

Strolling in Mormon's Mecca

Sevier River Valley in southwest Utah is narrow and curvy. That area possesses a sober and strange beauty at the end of winter. Snow is still abundant on the top of the hills. But the weather is not cold. The weather is even temperate. The landscape is maroon, brownish. Herds of sheep, horned cattle, and a few horses wander here and there on the muddy slopes and in the bottom of the valley. The animals are hairy, shaggy. Hair full of tangles. The habitat is old, mostly unrepaired and shaky. A hard wind would most probably put everything down like a row of card castles.

The drive along country Road 89 is increasingly monotonous. Many restaurants, snack bars and small businesses are closed. Garages are closed. Movie theaters are converted or closed.

Sevier River Valley is *du jamais vu*, difficult to describe. And that impressionnist perspective is valuable for most of the area extending from the state frontier, south, and Richfield and Thistle, north, close to Provo and the

Interstate Highway 15 leading rapidly to Salt Lake City. Shifting from the country road to the highway is just like passing from nighttime to daytime, from rural nineteenth century to triumphant modernity. A modernity which characterizes the sunny, very clean, well-designed, wealthy, over-devout, intolerant and boring Mormon's Mecca, I mean famous Salt Lake City!

I fry my pancakes right alongside the sidewalk, in the city center, where the Dodge van is parked at lunchtime, with a red hot sun throwing long flames high into the blue sky. The small snack takes place right after some strolling in Trolley Square, a must for browsers with a few bucks in their wallet. (I don't have much.) Massive spiritual power symbol, the white stones of the church of Jesus Christ Latter-Day Saints stand erect high on Temple Square.

The architecture of the quadrangular building is something quite special with its alternation of Roman and bull's-eye-shaped window alignments. The very slender spires of the six towers pierce the sky while an uninterrupted column of pilgrim ants move forward at a slow pace, ground level. Its white stones reflect the sun's rays with high intensity during the day, and the very slender steeples brilliantly alight during the night. Temple Square Church tells you twenty-four hours a day that you are in a proud, religious city.

Through a small-sized but authentic miracle

that gives a man's life sense, I meet Donna and her Doberman, Gypsy, later in the afternoon. In front of a row of houses to be demolished. From one thing to another and, from one place to another, we finally end up stranded near Chicago Street. A joyful game of tennis is played outdoors, late afternoon. Spicy spaghetti and red wine is served in a cosy place, Donna's place, during the first part of the evening, talking freely. What happens during the second part of the evening is not the reader's business.

I miss the world-famous 352-voice Tabernacle Choir by an inch, that night, but at 12:05 p.m., the very next day, a rigadoon — oh scandal! — plays full blast on the keyboard of the Tabernacle organ (equipped with 11,000 pipes, no less). On the road. On the road again. Salt Lake City, Spic and Span City as imperialistically oppressive as only Jerusalem and other religious centers can be, I leave you behind! But what are you doing here, Pedro? You, infidel to all kinds of faiths! You, lover of the earthy world and simple words, you are getting sucked in!

I am already crossing the town limits when I suddenly remember a guy I met in Frisco, whose family was established in Utah. He told me about his great-grandfather who had travelled west with Brigham Young. Had forty wives that lucky fellow.

Lucky?

Little Cow Gave Birth
to Three Kids

Ford Pala River at twilight on Cole Grade Road. These dry, sharp-angled mountains belong to southern California. Gold powder of the sunset, thin pastel mist over the ridges at the Occident. Slow down the van. Give others a chance, let the imperious traffic pass on the vehicle side. Slow down some more. The beauty of the whole world in a few moving moments, the evanescent beauty of the world, drunk from the cup of my hands.

After a half day off, I am returning to La Loreina Farm located at Valley Center, where I am practically in charge of the place for a couple of weeks. Ten or twelve people usually live there. But, of them, John, Luz and some kids are now travelling in the Hawaiian Islands. During this same period, Charlie and Anna are busy on the coast most of the time. La Loreina Farm is a tremendous estate which expands mostly along the side of the mountain and is covered mainly with avocado plants. The neighbors are also in the farming business. Avocados, grapefruits, oranges. From time to time, a couple of 'wetbacks' move swiftly like foxes behind trees, up the hills. That's right, they cross the border fraudulently. The Chicanos look for farmhand work.

The plantation expands mostly along the side of the mountain. Partly because it is a good location, partly because there is not much room at the bottom of the valley. The flats are more and more narrow as one goes down the valley, and the river itself is not tolerant at all. Especially at this time of year — it is mid-March — when the winter rains have been heavy. It harasses man and takes no rest. The river bites a big lump of land here, makes long crevices there, throws rocks in other places. It cuts across a loop of land, destroying its own banks, makes a curve, breaks its own curve and swings in the low open fields, containing precious orchards and gardens. An enormous crazy snake. The river spits and spins. The river is wild, out of bounds!

God bless us, Bill Kirst is there. Bill's farm is the next one down the stream. A sturdy man in his early fifties, he is a primitive warrior. Using as ammunition some 4,000 tires and metal nets, he creates solid obstacles to counter-attack the more violent fits of the vindicative stream.

'All year round, fighting erosion like it was a monster, yet he is a great lover of the river,' said Charlie, adding, 'and to my knowledge, a natural and very active poet.' For sure!

Lightly jumping on sand bars, being as an acrobat walking on a tightrope, I run over slippery dead trees, but mostly I just walk in a narrow trail between tall bushes and trees; almost every afternoon I can be found in the river valley. There's something wild here, something of the jungle. Maybe it's the dark green, maybe the discovery of mysterious shacks, abandoned dormitories for Chicanos. Maybe it's the silence — after a certain period of time, it becomes a little oppressive.

I return then to La Loreina, a long wooden stick in hand, the faithful black dog Uno trotting at my heels. Walking through the steep and very damp side of the hills, I watch the farm kids, left by the school bus at the top, already on their way home. I accelerate my pace. Time to cook another abundant supper for all of them.

There are fruit plantations on the farm, there are also bees and beehives. One day I worked with Charlie on the hot tin roof of the honey stock-and-tools warehouse. We were fixing shelves of corrugated metal eight feet long. We nailed the damned hot pieces for hours. The sun was merciless, but the valley breeze was good on our chins and shoulders. The many hours spent banging in nails ten feet from the ground, the euphoria of springtime, the talking and joking . . . A gust of wind brutally pulled from Charlie's hands a shining metal sheet. The devilish thing flew fast as a morning bird. Two inches closer to my red neck, not one more, and I would have suffered a first-class beheading. The thundering plate landed with a sinister, resounding *wham-m-m*.

Charlie was a really merry and witty character. Swift as the wind, he was also a highly ranked amateur jogger. As well as being a singer. One Sunday afternoon Charlie performed with the Escondido Oratorio Chorale. All the ladies in pink dresses, all the gentlemen in white taffeta tuxedos. The shirts even had frills! An astonishing show. Charlie was also a lawyer. In the dark days of the Vietnam War, he had been the first man of law in the United States to win a case dealing with the draft and with conscientious objectors, the first man of law to free a dodger from the very heavy hands of Justice.

A couple of days before the La Loreina people's trip to Hawaii came to an end, I had to go back to the Pacific Coast. Charlie surveyed things from afar, and some of the older kids were left alone for perhaps one day on the farm. That was during the weekend. On the Sunday I came back with friends from Cardiff: Conrad, Holly and the kids. In spite of the inspiring day, there was a wind of disaster blowing over La Loreina. The goats hadn't been milked; the hens hadn't been fed, nor had the dogs, the cats and the other animals on the farm. In a word, the teenagers had had a good time just fooling around. The three of us had to run like mad trying to put things back to normal. 'Our troubles are over now,' I said later to my companions with a smile.

As we were seated for lunch, Paul and Bret framed their very pale heads in the dining room door. Bret's shirt and shorts were torn. From shoulder to ankle, rows of black pebbles were incrusted in his skin. There were also small spots of blood here and there. Both kids had had an exciting run on their roller skates. Bret had come very near a heavy cropper speeding along the narrow asphalt road. According to Paul, Bret did a somersault and landed on the loose gravel flanking the road. Still chewing a piece of lettuce, I took Bret and Paul to my van. Spread out the first-aid kit on the floor: Band-Aids, little rolls of gauze, sample pots of ointment. Ridiculous. We walked back inside. I told Bret to stand up in the bath, told Paul to wash his friend's wounds with water and Ivory soap, asked Bret to swallow a couple of Aspirins, then resumed my lunch in the living room. I was almost finished the fruit salad when a young girl slammed the door open and said with a piercing voice: 'Little Cow is giving birth to its babies! Little Cow is giving birth to its babies!'

I ran to the goat's corral, a steaming cup of coffee in hand. The whole crowd followed. It was true: the big lady goat we call Little Cow already had one kid lying on the ground. I knelt down, helping her deliver two more.

Carefully put my hands a little ways inside. Good placenta heat on my skin. Holly gave me a hand. Little Cow licking the little faces of the kids in the sunlight, cleaned the mucus stuck in their mouths.

Our hands and arms were gluey with amniotic fluid. I milked the mother. A beautiful liquid, cream yellow, filled a small bucket. Unctuous cholesterum. Took a deep breath, smiled at Holly, then looked around.

At two o'clock in the afternoon, we were in the middle of a joyous country fair. Tall and small, something between fifteen and twenty people were watching the live show. An enthusiastic lady took some pictures. Jane, a young mother, was seated quietly nearby on the grass, suckling her child. At the very same moment, Holly was feeding the third little kid with a bottle in the goat's corral.

Early evening. Drive back to the Coast. I'll be driving eastbound soon. Thinking about my arrival day at La Loreina. Chased badgers in the avocado plantation. Feeling merry . . . The many drawings of the bridge I was supposed to build so easily over the creek. . . . The sketches of Becky and Meagan, the young girls. Tender . . . The joyous and peaceful dinner with Luz, the reigning queen, Michael, David, Paul, John, and all the others. Right afterwards, Meagan at the piano; John, a professional musician, a real artist, played the cello. What a beautiful melody . . . Wake up Pedro, you just came close to killing a rabbit! Stay in the here and now, brother. Better look at the dark, tricky road.

Bret is in the van, going home. It is just a short drive. Soon we arrive at the intersection of Santa Fe Boulevard. Bret steps down cautiously. He makes a phone call to his father, asks him to pick him up right here. The father says okay. I am in a hurry for a dinner appointment in Cardiff. Leave Bret where he is. Press on the gas pedal. I look at him for the last time: quiet, silent, Bret waits for Dad. He stands up on his roller skates, moves slowly, carefully. One movement towards the front, one movement towards the back, his long shadow dancing like an elf on the deserted highway. The telephone booth lighted by the roadside. Not a house in sight, no traffic, just complete darkness all around. The magic glowing blue of the night.

Bird Hunting
on the Seashore

To find Bolinas is not an easy task. The local
people regularly remove all the road signs
bearing the name of the place. This self-pro-
tected and very seclusive small town is located
right at the limit of Point Reyes National Sea-
shore, a short distance north of San Francisco.
Road signs or not, I found my way early in
December 1979. I didn't stay in Bolinas but
drove my van straight to the Bird Observatory
Station, a little further south. Spoke to some
station researchers who were observing and
counting birds in the surrounding bushes.

Fog and dampness were coming forth from
both the ocean and the nearby mountains. It
was dinnertime. David, Libby, Sally, John, Tom
and Steve invited me warmly to share their
meal. Which meant also to share in the cooking; and as cooking is a natural talent in my
case, I was kept very busy till everything was
served piping hot on the table. The same
agreeable ritual was to be reenacted every late
afternoon of my five-day sojourn at the Bird
Observatory Station. That was Monday.

On Tuesday, I went along with a couple of researchers to give them a hand catching birds. The biology students soon found a place among the thickets and set up vertical nets looking like the ones set in rivers' mouths to catch fish. Same principle. Here, the netting of birds was quite a success. After a while we counted three fox sparrows, one ruby-crowned kinglet and, finally, one red-breasted sapsucker. Quite a noisy and colorful crop! The birds had to be removed from the net and carried to the station for banding.

Removal of the birds from the net required very delicate hands. I did my best. I think that my heart was pounding almost as much as the birds', seeing them in that state of fright and panic. At one point in the badging operation, a yellow female warbler began crying — there's no other words to describe the distressing sound emitted, high-pitched and non-stop. Too painful to stand. I do not have the fowler's qualities and so went outside. And that was it for that first day.

Wednesday was a quiet day. While the team of the Bird Observatory Station kept itself busy with its scientific business, I walked for hours in the open fields and low bushy hills. On Palomarin Trail Head I saw a deer and, at twilight, four fowl on the road, the best time for wild animal watchers in this wild coastal land.

My Thursday journey to Point Reyes was quite well-prepared. I had even bought a detailed topographical map. Everybody was busy at the station, so I went alone. Lunch in a public park in Olema, all around tall, beautiful conifers, and the sun was warm. In the distance, a bunch of school kids surrounded by adults. I pitied them; they stood no chance of escaping in the bushes to play. Two black horses stared at me; I stared back at them. There were birds yelling in the pines as I cleaned the dishes: one bowl, one cup, one fork. I slid my pocket-knife back into my trousers. Time to go, the detailed topographical map of the Point Reyes area unfolded on the passenger's seat.

Drove the van on the so-called Sir Francis Drake Highway, which in fact is a narrow, winding country road. Climatic ocean influence all over. There was no more sun. Windy, gray, and the incoming fog was moving fast. Suddenly I saw a herd of cattle crossing the wet road. Pushed hard on the brake pedal near Rogers Ranch, where a muddy herd of cows passed right in front of the van. A sturdy fellow wearing a heavy winter coat with a sheep lining opened and closed the gates. His rough face returned no smile in answer to my wave.

Windy, raining, a terrible dampness. The light of Point Reyes was quite near now. A couple of rangers, a boy and a girl dressed in their Boy Scout uniforms, chatted in a small shack. Three hundred steps down to the lighthouse. I have never had to walk *down* when visiting a lighthouse. I put both my elbows on the railing that bordered the steep cliff and adjusted my binoculars so as to spot the gray whales on their way to the breeding shores of Baha California. I was anxious to see them but didn't. Perhaps my eyes were not imaginative enough to differentiate a whale's spout from the water's foam. And as for sea lions, there were none basking on the offshore rocks: none on stage today. It'll be for next time.

No whales, no sea lions, only a sail boat from ancient times moved quickly over the fierce waves. Was it Drake's 'Golden Hinde' or Sebastian Rodriguez Cermeno's 'San Agustin'? Difficult to determine when you are not an ancient sail boat specialist! In such a climate I bet that it was the Spanish explorer out there because Cermeno came in these parts during the winter. The Englishman Drake, Queen Elizabeth's intimate friend, had come during summertime. The curtain of rain had thickened. I felt it was wise to leave right then, even though I did not believe in ghosts.

Nothing particular happened on Friday morning. I spent the afternoon in the surrounding Bolinas Lagoon which expands beautifully inland. Green grass in December. The Dodge van was parked on the roadside. A 'real' farm nearby, the only one around, to my memory. There were many painted stones in the fields, shades of brown, which started to move: the heads of cattle, a playful calf among them. A few horses stood still, close to the farmhouse. Crows were discussing their personal business aloud. On the lagoon a duck and a lonely white bird. The midday sun, fiery on my temples and forehead.

The dark greens of Bolinas Ridge spread a few hundred yards in the background. A narrow, tortuous, steep road ran between Wilkins Gulch and Pike Country Gulch. I turned the ignition off, pulled the hand brake and walked in the conifers towards the cliffs. The insects danced in the light. I kept still and drank the sun to the last drop. Pocket watch in hand, I looked at the ocean, at the bottom of the cliffs, everywhere, and absorbed the whole landscape before sundown; a time full of grave majesty stretched its seriousness over the conifers.

Right after dinner I went to 'Horseshoe Drive', an opulent mansion located at the town limits. There was an announcement pinned on the outside wall of the Bolinas food store about a musical performance to be held at the mansion. Big American cars, expensive, but without the smallest touch of personality, grace or beauty in design, crowded the alleys. Here and there, a Fiat, a B.M.W., a Jaguar. Parochial ladies' morning club spirit inside. Aleudin Mathieu, the pianist, came in dressed like a dandy in white and pastel tones, a smiling, happy puppet. The show got underway, the performer pinching the chords of the open piano and touching everything but the keys. People were ecstatic. Aleudin Mathieu is the most authentic barnstormer that I have seen or heard of in my life. A real artist in every distorted sense of the word.

Behind me a wide fireplace was consuming entire trees, so warm that my corduroy jeans smelled scorched. Didn't move, couldn't move, squeezed as I was among well-washed, well-perfumed, well-dressed ladies and gents. Head turning with a crackle in the neck. I fixed on the lights of San Francisco flickering and twinkling over the panoramic windows of the 'Horseshoe Drive' mansion, which kept me cool until intermission time.

The sky was gray on Saturday, the weather for the weekend quite poor. The possibility of sharing a house for several weeks with some people connected with the Bird Observatory Station had been discussed during the week. Good time to visit the place in the morning. A charming site on Overlook Road in Bolinas. Upon careful reflection, I decided I wasn't in the mood to live here or in any other place. Later on I was proven wrong, but we won't get into that right now. As there was nobody around at that time of the day, I left a message on the kitchen table: '*Tried to settle down. Impossible. The wind is stronger than the walls.*'

At slow speed on tortuous Road 1. Full speed on Freeway 101. Medium speed amid

the traffic on the Golden Gate Bridge. At night.
In the rain. I felt like a wet bird.

Chicanos Caught Early
in the Rain

In the second half of the nineteenth century, Calistoga was full of male Chinese servants: cooking, washing, gardening, driving horse carriages for the wealthy Californians living there and nearby. Those guys were quite busy. But times have changed. In December, 1979, I met only one, who came periodically from San Francisco to collect money. He was the owner of the place where I had rented half a puppet-sized bungalow, on Anna Street. And there was a whole village of those bungalows covered with old white planks, right in the middle of town. Chicanos — workers in the surrounding vineyards — filled them all, save for my half-bungalow; and the lady manager of the whole thing came from Columbia in South America. We were then a kind of league of nations down in the dead end of Napa Valley, which is Calistoga.

The first night of 'sleep' in my small-scale shelter had been an unforgettable nightmare. Soft bed, dry nose, cockroaches! At six in the morning, the Chicanos were all awake. The crude light of the electric bulbs was piercing in the darkness. The babies, the mammas, the school-aged children, the workers boosting their damp trucks in the cold rain, everyone had something to say in Spanish. Then in a very insidious way came daylight. A dishwater daylight of a rainy winter. At seven the male Chicanos were all gone. Piled, stuck, cramped in the rear boxes of the small trucks. Most days, because of the constant heavy rain, the straw-hatted guys returned shortly to fool around for the rest of the day.

From the bay window of the living room, I could see kids playing games and tricks for hours around a lonely tree keeping still in the mud. Here and there along the bare branches crumpled yellow leaves hung sadly. Sometimes in the morning, by pure miracle, a miserly sun appeared, teasing me with its golden ball dancing in the small open space between the low buildings bordering the sides of the yard. In the afternoon, when we were lucky, the sun emerged for a few minutes out of the big fluffy gray rolling clouds and lit the table. The table for eating, the table for writing.

I opened the portable typewriter box. A sheet of white paper was still fixed in the typing roll. An eye half closed, I read, *Wind stronger than the walls. Flying hobo is burning the roads.*

The kitchen window was not as wide open as the one facing the front, but it gave a view of the fields, with a *vue imprenable*, newspaper ads written in French would have said. The real estate sales argument was used in good fashion: an airfield was located just beside the fence, a few yards from the back of my bungalow. And that airfield was a nest for gliders. Most days, the flying structures lay flat on the wet strips and surrounding area. Wet ducks dripping. But on any of the few sunny days of the long winter, the gliders, pulled by small airplanes, took to the air, becoming silver and dorado albatrosses and gulls.

Not the least famous Mount Saint Helena filled half of the background. I climbed it once. A climb late in the afternoon. Found myself caught by darkness in the damp forest. No flashlight but a lot of wooden matches. I had previously grabbed, by instinct, a whole pile of pamphlets describing the natural marvels of Robert Louis Stevenson's State Park where I was supposed to be, so the situation was not really one of despair. A couple of pamphlets were lit in a jiffy. Brandishing my Roman torch, arm raised high, I proceeded along the narrow trail. Flames danced like elves on the dark dripping trees.

The forest was almost silent, except for a pine cone falling on a bed of needles with a little 'tick', or the faint gurgle of a small brook finding its way down over some rocks covered with moss. *Hooboo* . . . *Hooboo* . . . A great owl glided between the trees, bringing the mysterious close to the horrifying. The atmosphere was not serene, but funereal, dismal, gloomy. A few more yards in the ghost kingdom and the blazing pamphlets illuminated a sculptured stone. The upper part was cut and shaped to resemble an open book lying flat. The purpose of the tombstone-like monument was to remind passers-by that Robert Louis Stevenson had spent his honeymoon right here, summer 1880, living in an old miner's shack.

Seeing the stone gave me a violent chill up and down my spine. The mountain air had supposedly given the writer, dying of tuberculosis, fourteen more years to live, travel, write, publish. Honeymoon here, really? Why not, for a genuine Scottish tartan guy at ease since birth with mist and rain over Lowlands and Highlands, with sheep, ruined castles and men, the raging rain giving them its grays, maroons, and greens, the most poetic feeling and spleen! Thanks anyway, Robert, for having been so famous in your time that a state park's pamphlet, dealing with your simple stay here with a lady, would be published and exist in my time. I grabbed a whole bunch of those pamphlets to light my way down Mount Saint Helena, straight towards a steaming stew simmering in the kitchen oven in my own solitary cabin.

The terrible rain ruled picturesque, up-to-date California for long, wet, dark weeks, north and south. One day, radio news caught from

Portland, Oregon, announced that, following heavy rains and floods, blackouts and major losses were recorded everywhere on the West Coast and inland. For example, in Baja California, a rough and remote vast region which belongs to Mexico, a lot of bridges simply split and broke. Monotonous litany to be read in the newspapers: Tecate-Ensenada road cut at seven places; Ensenada-San Quentin road cut in five places in 120 miles; San Quentin-El Rosario road cut in three places.

Two American cars filled with American tourists tried to ford a creek transforming itself, from minute to minute, into a thundering water avalanche stuffed with boulders and rocks. At first they floated but then they rushed along in the wild muddy currents, turning and spinning just like little chips of wood. As I listened to and read about the horror show, I just had to forget my idea of rolling down to Baja California next springtime. As consolation prize, I had the benefit of a genuine Latin atmosphere right over here, with each and every Chicano yelling from dawn to twilight.

I wanted to make them be quiet, like me. My pretention, to want to shut their mouths. To cool them off. Make them get up on their tip-toes in the morning. I hated them but I envied them also. At night, I used to walk in the Chicanos' village, peering through the puppet-sized bungalow windows. Whole tribes were gathered around the tables for supper.

Radio loudspeaker. From hour to hour, news in Spanish. People chatted, teased each other, discussed, gesticulated, ate, drank, and looked at color TVs. Protected from the night and the rain, the Chicanos seemed to be happy. There were no telephones in the bungalows, and it took me a long time to understand the meaning of the numerous children moving from house to house, from door to door. The niños were carrying invisible messages.

Sometimes, after finishing my writing, usually in the afternoon, I would jump in the van and fly away from the Chicanos' close environment. On one of those dull afternoons in the rain, I got stranded at Angwin, a few miles east, near Lake Berryessa. Wealthy campus. Kind of college. Training center for Seventh Day Adventists. The heads of the students, the heads, my God! Insipid, insignificant, vacuous faces. No color, no natural beauty. Face-washed, brainwashed in Javex solution. Short hair, harsh hair, brush cut convict-style, or flat with brilliantine for the brave boys, the most plain and conventional style for the girls.

Sick northern people. Many of them are here to become missionaries around the world. Were I an African native, I would poison their Kellogg's Corn Flakes straight off. Oh; what now! A whole flock of freshly arrived Filippino girls, satchels, umbrellas and so on, are walking along the side of the van, smiling, joking, laughing. How long until they too will be thrown into the Javex solution by their masters and mistresses? Anxious.

Calistoga was advertising itself as the Hot Springs of the West, displaying a wide range of hot mineral water pools, mud and steam baths. One afternoon, I paid a visit to Old Faithful. He is not a prophet; he is not an old man; he is a geyser. As advertised, 'a geyser erupting from the earth in all its beauty and splendor.' We were ten silly people trampling in the mud and waiting in religious silence for the splendor to come, for the next puff of steam shot by Old Faithful. The tourists shivering in the rain prepared their cameras, ready to shoot and film. Gripped between my teeth, my pipe was blowing blue smoke.

Finally it came! Gurgling like the drain of the curved pipes of a kitchen sink in deep trouble, a weak and stinky 'jet' popped up out of a swampy hole. There was enough steam to press three pairs of pants or to supply a Turkish bath for about thirty seconds. And my tobacco pipe was extinguished because of the stinky damp atmosphere created by damned Old Faithful.

Cut off by the mountains at Calistoga, Napa Valley grows the best grapes in California — which means the best grapes in the United States, which also means the best in North America. And as I am a wine drinker, if not a wine connoisseur, I was surely on good ground in the Napa Valley. Calistoga, my base for the winter, along with Napa itself, Rutherford, and Saint Helena, the next village south, produce the finest of the finest of table wines.

In December 1979, when I was heading for Calistoga, I made a stop in the afternoon at Joseph Phelps Vineyards in Saint Helena. That was a few days before the rainy season. Sky and landscape were mellow. Sweet and sour melancholy of the autumn filled the air. Memories of western Europe a persistent feeling. Beautiful place and fine hosts. I was offered delicate flutes of white nectar. I can still see an opalescent Johannisberg Riesling 1976; I can still savor its fruity velvet. I also see a bottle of Le Fleuron 1978. *Vin blanc* was written in French on the label. White wines of Napa Valley, quiet snow of clear delight.

In January, a few days before my departure from Calistoga's Chicano village, I bought a simple, low-priced Zinfandel de Mondavi at Saint Helena's grocery store. I drank the bottle just about in front of the low flat land where the grapes had matured. That wine was a jewel, a ruby glowing in spite of the monotonous rain. Yes, a simple bottle of wine, drunk with respect, drunk with love for the land, for all the good people I had met in town — and they were many! — during my sojourn, for the Chicanos and the wine brains of Napa Valley. I drank also — and it was time because the bottle was almost empty — with love for the

Gods for having given us, men and women, the sumptuous richness of wine.

Disney World
and the Golden Age

Their pink panties alternatively shown then hidden in rhythm, the French cancan girls kick the Californian sky with plastic smiles. The attractive performers are dancing on a motorized platform preceeded by an oversized teddy bear wagging his stupid head. The rolling stage is followed by a group of supposedly comic clowns. Next comes a pair of enormous but peaceful horses, hauling — *clap clap clap* — the steam music of a steamboat. Shining trumpets, bass, cornets, slide trombones, a powerful band playing the musical theme of the homecoming parade: 'We are one big family.' I am at Hermosa Beach in L.A. in 1980.

That year Disneyland celebrated its '25th Family Reunion'. Monorail speeding along, red bus straight from London rolling through the alleys, firemen pulling the bell-rope of a fire-engine also rolling along, musical sounds, roarings, yellings, the atmosphere is electrical. I buy a row of tickets. Big Thunder Mountain Railroad, Haunted Mansion, Sky to Tomorrowland, Tom Sawyer Land, Small World presented by the Bank of America, time goes fast when you're having fun! 'The happiest place on earth' is really crowded. So crowded that, to absorb the permanently growing flock of visitors, the engineers have had to viciously speed up the machinery of the attractions, a friend who had been born just nearby explained to me. Waiting lines are also set in a zigzag pattern so as to make people move and remain patient.

After having spent more than half of my tickets, I take it easy, in between America Sings, presented by Del Monte Canned Fruits, and Buddy Rich & The Buddy Rich Band, on Plaza Gardens. Stroll sloppy style on Main Street U.S.A. Neat, neat, neat.

When I started working on Disneyland my wife used to say, 'Why do you want to build an amusement park? They're so dirty!' I told her that was just the point: mine wouldn't be. Guess who said that? Spic and span fairyland, giant set of celluloid toys, life-like smart plastic stuff, no microbes, aseptic, a real fun lab!

Sun is tough today. Got to find some free shade somewhere. The Walt Disney Story is featuring 'Great moments with Mr. Lincoln' — presented by the Gulf Corporation. Presidential human-scale puppets stand next to the hall were the Seventh Amendment is framed on the wall. And if you have forgotten, reader, the Seventh Amendment is the cool classical apology of free enterprise. Amiable chat with Iranians near the Gulf Oil presentation. Nade, Shayda and Tahir are Persians nowadays.

Walt Disney's childish, mercantile recreation of Mecca left an imperishable image in my memory. The one of the Golden Age and otherwise respectable people fighting like little kids just in front of the attraction. First, to get a place. Second, to get the best one. That reminds me of something. Was watching the Mother Goose Parade with delight in El Cajun, on Sunday the 18th of November, 1979. Marching bands were very good. Majorettes: slim, smart and pretty girls. Then came many very tall men in their sixties, wearing red violet tarboosh adorned with swinging tassels. Acting joyously like kids — but with all physiognomical stigmas of the elderly, deep-pocketed eyes and so on — the old timers were having a good time driving small-scale motorized fire-engines and cars, right in the middle of Main street. With spectators standing along the sides. With real kids standing and looking, amazed but puzzled.

The Last Picture Show

About a week before the Fourth of July celebration. Texarkana, a frontier town between Arkansas and Texas. Driving on Freeway 30 southwest to Dallas. Eighty miles in the swift traffic, then find a KOA camping ground in time to put an end to an exhausting journey. We settle for the night. I say 'we' because a ladyfriend and her twelve-year-old daughter are travelling with me for a while. We fix the tent and relax. I check our geographical location on the road map. Sixty miles northwest is Paris, Texas. About five miles south, Mount Pleasant.

After dinner, eaten on a picnic table, we all decide to explore the place. Short drive at twilight. Mount Pleasant is a ghost town at this hour of the day. Nobody walking, nobody driving, nobody. A small old place. Remote in time and space. We roll slowly. No words. Looking at everything with a growing feeling of strangeness. I wonder if the movie *The Last Picture Show* was shot here. On our way back to the camping ground, we make a quick stop to pass the time at a small snack bar standing close to Freeway 30.

Two vehicles are parked in front. A sedan and a pickup truck. Seated in the car, a light black couple in their mid-thirties. They just sit there, sweating in the night. In the pickup, two Winchesters are hung on hooks at the back of the cabin. *Easy Rider*, local version, I say to my ladyfriend with a sour smile. The three of us casually enter the small snack bar. A comfortable, well-kept place. Air-conditioned, of course. The owner, a man in his fifties, is busy counting meal slips beside the counter while his wife can be seen and heard moving pots about in the kitchen.

We soon order coffee, a soft drink and pie à la mode. The neat place is almost empty. Two customers — the people from the pickup — are seated diagonally across from our own table. Booted, burly fellows with cowboy hats worn flat on the top of their heads. Big red heads adorned with side-whiskers. Those two burly fellows are staring at us. They have already had their coffee and they are just staring at us. Watching the slightest motion of the hand and the fork. Watching and listening to everything. And they stay still, just staring at us.

It is only when I have swallowed my last mouthful that I notice such a peculiar attitude. The atmosphere is now heavy in the snack bar. You could hear a fly had there been any. Oh God! I realize what's wrong. My ladyfriend is white but Nathalie, her beautiful twelve-year-old daughter, is black. Furthermore, her black hair is triumphantly cut in an afro, which is provocative at the best of times. I walk to the counter. I pay my bill, spotted with drops of sweat in spite of a well-running climatization system.

We move out. I feel tense. Then the two burly fellows move out too. They give us a last cool glance and jump in their pickup truck, quickly leaving the place. They have won on one good point: we had to scram out of the snack bar before they would leave. They had a clear lead in the situation. And the cool and officially polite attitude of the owners of the small restaurant no doubt also expressed hostility. At least, they were not on our side.

All this time I have forgotten about the black couple seated in the sedan car. They are still there. As soon as the pickup truck leaves the parking lot, they go inside. Professionally curious, I turn off the ignition in the Dodge van, walk a few yards and peer through a window. The black man and the black woman are seated. They are sipping orange juice. Orange juice . . . Risking their life for a glass of cold refreshment. Nonsense.

The ladyfriend, her daughter, and I roll back to KOA camping site, and we all go to sleep in the precarious shelter of the cloth, in a fragile blue tent. But I can't sleep. I am thinking about Nathalie, the burly fellows, and the people living nearby. I am saying to myself: the people from the snack bar, the camping ground management and maintenance people, they are most probably from the surrounding counties and towns. Maybe they all think the same way about the right things for whites to do and the right things for blacks. Then I have a flashback about Mount Pleasant in the twilight. I become seriously afraid that some Ku Klux Klansmen, led by the two burly fellows, will come silently during the night. Should I move my two-toned, very recognizable van, parked just beside the tent, and clean up the place? I finally sleep because I am so tired, and we leave, Dallas-bound, quite early in the morning.

The affair-that-never-happened in the snack bar took place late in June. A few months later, alone this time, I was somewhere in New Mexico. Bought the Sunday newspaper, the *Albuquerque Journal*. Two dramatic news items were placed together in the same article:

Greensboro, N.C. (UPI) - Five people were killed and nine wounded as Ku Klux Klansmen leaped from a van and began shooting at a group staging an anti-Klan march through a black neighborhood Saturday, authorities said.

The gun battle in Greensboro coincided with a tense Klan march in Dallas, where hundreds of riot-equipped police protected about 50 Klan marchers. One of the officers said tensions were so high he was amazed a riot did not erupt.

'That is Dallas, that is north Texas, that is the classic black-and-white troubled area. Just forget about it. We are different down here. Instead of loafing around at a roadside snack bar and driving through what seems to be a ghost town in north Texas, why don't you try a small-town Texan barbecue?' my interlocutor was saying. Wearing a cowboy hat and booted, like the burly Winchester fellows but smiling full-face. The benevolent Southerner even recommended the two meccas of central Texas barbecue. First, 'Louis Mueller' in Taylor, on U.S. Highway 79, between Temple and Austin. Second, 'Kreuz Market' in Lockhart, on U.S. Highway 183, thirty miles south of Austin.

Yes, a boneless prime rib with all the trimmings, jalapeño peppers, avocado and beer. What a treat! One day, I will step over the threshold of meat mecca, pass along the open pit among the hungry crowd, get into line at the rounded counter where orders are taken, get my rib slapped onto pink butcher paper and weighed. Then I will sit in the smoky atmosphere of the good old times with everyone taking pleasure in eating the juicy and well-seasoned barbecued beef flesh. Already salivating, I suddenly wonder if Nathalie who proudly exhibits her afro would be offered the same welcome. I really wonder . . .

112

The Lopez,
My Sanchez Family

Taos Pueblo, New Mexico.

'May I climb to the top?'

'No!' roughly answered a high school boy who was chatting with two girls near the Morning Talk Indian Shop.

I had intended, using ladders fixed along the outside wall, to climb to the top of the two- or three-storied adobe building. No time, no place to argue. Turning my back on the trio, I walked towards a clear mountain creek rushing down on the rocks. A mountain creek most probably mixing its cool flow with Arroyo Aguaje de la Petaca, a few miles west and, not too far away, with the waters of the famous Rio Grande. Contemplating the narrow crystalline river, I cleaned my eyes to refresh my mind and looked at the beautiful blue sky.

Right after a hard drive on a narrow road — overflowing with nervous pilots driving noisy cars — such a quiet interlude was an absolute necessity. Had been jammed in front of Kit Carson Memorial in Taos for several long minutes. According to my memories of movies seen in my childhood, I thought that he was a star cowboy. But things must be readjusted to fit the truth. Kit Carson Memorial refers to militia colonel Christopher Carson who became very famous more than a century ago by severely beating the Indians and subduing them forever. First, the Mescalero Apaches. Second, the Navahoes. Coming on stage with the brutal power of the Juggernaut, he proceeded to systematically destroy the Indian crops, confiscate the livestock, and, for its scale, most probably as deadly as the Bataan Death March, plan and carry out the Long Walk towards Bosque Redondo.

New Mexico has always been a thundering merry-go-round for fighting. So, why should I react as if scandalized? For centuries, long before the arrival of the whites, the Indian tribes fought one another. Then they fought with the Spaniards. The French fought later on with the Mexicans, and the latter with the Americans, who, after their victory, proceeded to decisively beat all the Indian tribes. Americans fought Americans in the Civil War and the Glorietta Pass Battle was honored as 'the Gettysburg of the West'. Another kind of civil war was also fought between shepherds and cattlemen. And cattle barons fought with each other.

A little more abstract but equally cruel fights broke out when land speculators and railroad 'corporators' fought to grab and keep the land. Around the same time Jewish-German and Yankee merchants fought to develop small and big businesses, and one must not forget the entrepreneurs from the mines and the industries fighting to possess their share of the natural wealth of New Mexico. And so on up to the dying of thousands and thousands of descendants from all the groups mentioned, whatever their color or faith, in the two world wars of the twentieth century. Finally, what can one say about the egg-heads reunited from all over, doing some heavy thinking in Los Alamos Ranch School on the Pajarito Plateau of the Jémez Mountains, concocting their hot cherry, which was tested in Trinity Site, White Sands, July 16, 1945.

On the fourth of November 1979, I slept in Las Cruces. On the fifth, in Santa Fe, on the sixth in Espanola, the next day in Medanales, then I was out of New Mexico, westbound for the far-advanced and Promised Land of California. In the first place I met Maria, a charming lady member of the family, the clan, the tribe of the Lopez. She gave me names, addresses and even phone numbers of somewhere around a dozen brothers and sisters living in different places in the western half of the country. And that is why, following my little visit to Taos Pueblo, I went straight to Espanola.

There lives Alexandro Lopez, a sensible and talented woodcarver. His brother Manuel, living nearby in Santa Cruz, also a woodcarver, came in later on. Forgetting about the rain and the muddy landscape, we talked and drank for hours inside. Looking at the sober and even severe indoor environment, at the well-crafted pieces of rustic furniture, and speaking Spanish, we could have been living at that very moment in Spain, in Mexico, or somewhere farther south.

But judging from some of the fine genuine personages and figures carved in the wood, we could also have been among European artists. There was the elongated extreme of Giacometti's sculptures, there was the primitive, archaic vein of Brancusi's sculptures, there was the mystical exaltation of Greco's paintings. The mother of all the Lopez, a fair and wise lady, was seated in a rocking chair, with all the bambinos running and fooling around. Peering through the window facing the road, we could see the small Catholic cemetery where her husband rested in peace.

Alfred Lopez, brother of Alexandro and Manuel, lives in Medanales. The seventh of November I was there and my van was parked in the yard. Alfred works at the Meson facility and is involved in medical research, at Los Alamos. His house stands in a remote area along Rio Chama. Stiff from all the driving of the previous days, wet from the walking and the cooking in the rain, really dirty, I was dreaming about a tub filled to the rim with steaming water; and I got it! Relaxed, refreshed, ready to jump on the road, in the dirt, again, but this time clean, I walked into the living room. '*Yo tengo tantos hermanos*' (I have so many brothers) was sung by the moving voice of Mercedes Sosa. A beautiful line was written on the record cover: *La cancion, el poeta y el hombre* (The song, the poetry of man). Then inspired, I walked outside to change clothes in the van.

Heard the wiz-wiz of the heavily loaded trucks on the road, not too far away. Looked at the scrubby vegetation. Observed the vastness of the land. New Mexico: the terrible cold of the night, the white snow shining on the mountain tops, the purity of the air, the clarity of optical vision, but also, the awful, contradictory, violent, dispersed gesture of human ants. And that creature is not one of peace. Worried to be, worried to be recognized, worried to know more, worried to take, build and control. I am a very worried creature. To ease my mind, I stood still, looking at the snow-covered mountains shining on the crude blue sky.

Optical play flavored by a pinch of imaginative powder, the thirty-six perspectives of Mount Fuji San engraved by Hokusai start turning like a very inspiring merry-go-round with some birds singing aloud in the bushes growing out of the dry land. 'Travelling in spirit,' I go back to the church of Saint Francis de Assisi in Rancho de Taos, where I was two days ago.

An oasis in the crazy circus of wealth, hedonism, and frantic motion that triumphs all around Santa Fe. But a church is not a place to live. The hot tub, the moving song of Mercedes Sosa, the vision of Hokusai's engravings, all those things are also oases that grace a worried man's road. A road traced amid its own crazy circus.

Springtime Is Born Among Farm Animals

This morning I find fresh light snow spread on the mountain slopes. We are in early springtime. I am ready to leave Boulder, Colorado. Turn on the radio. Barreling the van's engine. News bawls on an AM channel. The aborted attempt to free the hostages in Teheran is the feature of the talk show with its high-pitched voices. Of a task force comprised of eight helicopters, one had to go back quickly on the 'Nimitz' because its team felt dizzy. A second one landed in the desert because of mechanical problems and, later on, so did a third one. In the complete darkness, on the liftoff to go back home after the try, a fourth chopper and a C-13 plane collided. Both were engulfed in flames while a bunch of privates got roasted on board.

Quickly turn the radio off. Transmission shifted into low gear. Get the vehicle free from a muddy grade road. I am headed for Chicago, so today will be Nebraska State Day. A long drive ahead. Dark green color and square shape, a few spots of greenish vegetation strongly contrast with the gray of the winter landscape. Seven Corvettes moving Indian file, all different in their metallic colors, fly away from a rest area the moment I drop in.

Many herds, hundreds and hundreds of long- and short-horned beasts are spread over the countryside. All that livestock will be processed into roast beef, sirloin, T-bones, and hamburger steak in the slaughterhouses of big cities. That bloody image does not make me feel hungry. Only one bird in the sky, but I am happy to see freight trains on the horizon line again after having had to live for many weeks where there were none. One of them is carrying coal. To Denver, most likely. Brown and gray tones dominate the landscape all around. Such drab tints are not the colors for me! The sun, a hard copper disk, is setting quickly. Drink wine to balance the chilly weather. Evening drive. York. About sixty miles before entering Lincoln. Park the van for the night.

Leaden sky in the morning. Cold. I reach Lincoln by ten. In spite of a *froid de canard*, rose-colored flower buds are studded all over the rows of bushes facing Nebraska's state capitol. Well-trimmed bushes border a classical fountain. The town has an old scale, a human scale. But I am on a fast run today. I quickly move towards Omaha. Small picturesque city center. Not many people outside, not much traffic for a Saturday morning. I cross the bridge over Missouri River. Beyond is Iowa.

The greenish countryside pushes back in my memory shaggy and dusty Nebraska (pardon me, fellows of Nebraska!). Des Moines. The sun is shining on a big wedding cake. That's the state capitol. Greek pediment and bulbous towers of Slavic influence, all covered in gold braid. A surprising kind of architecture. You either like it or you don't. I do.

Straight east on Interstate 80. Travelling inside the grain belt of North America, a belt I've read about in old school books. Most cities are signaled on flat ground by wide railroad marshalling yards flanked with high rectangular grain silos. Rolling hills. Many birds. Tilled land, not as dark as yesterday. A few trees have their first leaves. Light-colored farmhouses, predominantly maroon and white. Silver silos popping up over the horizon line bring company to the spruce buildings. Curvy landscape. No wrong note outside, no wrong note inside.

Van's engine is humming well. Weather has warmed up since yesterday. Thousands of calves, thousands of lambs, crowds of pigs moving all around in the fields and between the fences. No doubt. What I am now seeing might as well be taken for granted. Nature's annual springtime show is on! The starting season of the annual cycle has already begun to bring good things to the American land, my land. Let's forget about blackbird's croonies of television and radio. Let's gain back confidence in life. Let's open wide the doors of expectation.

The afternoon has gone. Drive for hours under a thick roof of clouds. Then suddenly I'm no longer rolling under that roof. Have just passed the square-angled side of it. A brilliant sun lies right over the whitish, nebulous surface. So there's me running northeast along the road, and there's the sun moving southwest along the cloud's carpet. The bizarre phenomenon is exciting. Push hard on the gas pedal so as not to lose the sun's reflection on the van's side mirror. The eight big cylinders are giving everything they've got. Wind waves singing on the Dodge's square body. Successful for almost half an hour. Then suddenly lose track of the golden rolling ball. Take it easy on the gas pedal.

The dark of night has come. A few stars are shining. Eat the usual filling and, by my standards, satisfying dinner at Truck Stop 76. More than fifty motionless trucks are parked in the yard, diesel engines running slowly just like well-fed cats purring on armchairs. Light smell of gas and burnt oil. Quiet hour. A scrambled moon floats over the place. Feel good here. Feel at home. I am a motorized hobo.

By the Same Author

L'Homme essentiel
(Essays, 1975)

L'Homme gratuit
(Essays, 1977)

L'Homme éclaté
(Essays, 1984)

La Terre émue
(Poetry, 1986)

Le Diable au marais
(Fables, 1987)

- Cap-Saint-Ignace
- Sainte-Marie (Beauce)
Québec, Canada
1996

«L'IMPRIMEUR»